Her chalk white skin went even whiter.

"My God," Nashima said, "I should have known it would be a mistake to call on David Hawk."

"And what is that supposed to mean?"

"It means," she said, looking up at me with tears in her lovely eyes, "that I have signed my death warrant by calling David Hawk. You, Mr. Holmes—otherwise known as Nick Carter—are to be the instrument of my death."

NICK CARTER IS IT!

"Nick Carter out-Bonds James Bond."
—*Buffalo Evening News*

"Nick Carter is America's #1 espionage agent."
—*Variety*

"Nick Carter is razor-sharp suspense."
—*King Features*

"Nick Carter is extraordinarily big."
—*Bestsellers*

"Nick Carter has attracted an army of addicted readers . . . the books are fast, have plenty of action and just the right degree of sex . . . Nick Carter is the American James Bond, suave, sophisticated, a killer with both the ladies and the enemy."
—*The New York Times*

FROM THE NICK CARTER
KILLMASTER SERIES

A Killmaster Spy Chiller

NICK CARTER

THE CHRISTMAS KILL

ACE CHARTER BOOKS, NEW YORK

Dedicated to the men of the
Secret Services of the
United States of America

ONE

It was all over but the wrapup. And it looked increasingly certain that I would be the one to be wrapped up, not the gang of terrorists that lay waiting in a stand of trees between me and the beach.

The boat the Navy had provided lay bobbing in the water, not a hundred feet offshore. I had only to get down off the ledge, high above the Pacific Ocean on Colombia's western shore, swim out to the boat and pilot it to the submarine.

I had come to this section of Colombia a week ago to eliminate the leaders of an M19 group that had splintered off from the main force with plans to kill every American living in that South American country.

It had taken five days to kill the leaders. Miraculously, I had done it without sustaining personal injury, although Wilhelmina, my faithful and deadly accurate Luger had a large hunk taken out of her bone handle.

The theory, supplied by David Hawk from his safe little office on Dupont Circle in Washington, was that the terrorists would disband when the leaders went to Valhalla.

The theory was all wet. The terrorists had cornered me two days ago on this crummy ledge as I had descended the mountain just south of Bahia Octaria. Behind me was an open meadow where I could be picked off by the worst shot in the group. I was out of ammo, out of food, out of energy and, from the looks of things, out of luck.

I was just starting to whittle a spear with Hugo, my trusty stiletto—planning a do-or-die break for the small boat off the beach—when I heard the mutter of helicopter rotors from far out over the Pacific.

Below, sixty terrorist heads turned to the sky. As my own blue eyes scanned the darkening horizon, I spotted a huge black Bell Cobra. The pilot was as good with weapons as he was with the cyclic pitch and collective pitch controls that ran the Cobra. He swept the stand of trees, driving the terrorists into the open, firing up with rifles that had suddenly turned puny against this larger adversary.

Cowering against the ledge to keep from getting hit by the stray rockets, cannon shells and fifty-caliber machine gun bullets, I watched the incredible slaughter of sixty human beings. Men died amid screams of agony. Blood turned the white sand ochre. Bile rose in my throat and I vomited. I had to keep reminding myself that those sixty, given the chance, would have filled me with bullets and strung my entrails over a long section of beach.

When there was no further movement on the

beach, the Cobra swept back and forth three more times, then set down. A bull horn blared in the dusk.

"You up there. Are you Nick Carter?"

I cupped my hands over my mouth and shouted back. "Yeah, I'm Nick Carter. Who are you?"

"I have orders for you, Mr. Carter," the impersonal bull horn rumbled over the still, dead bodies of the M19 splinter group. "Come on down."

Once in the copilot's seat, I was handed a manila envelope. "Hold them so I can't read them," the pilot's gruff voice said.

With that, he snapped on a high intensity light that shone directly in my lap. He twisted the throttle control, eased back on the collective pitch stick and we lifted off. The pilot jammed forward the cyclic pitch stick and we whizzed out over the darkening ocean, taking a northerly tack toward Nicaragua.

I opened the envelope and removed a single sheet. It was a scrawled note from David Hawk, my boss. At the top was the coded designation, deciphering to "Nick Carter, Agent N3, AXE." In plain English and large type were the words: "HIS EYES ONLY." The note said: "You're out of the frying pan, but don't rejoice. The fire comes next—in Hiroshima, Japan."

The Cobra swept out to sea just short of Nicaragua's waters. The *Constellation* lay past the two hundred-mile limit Nicaragua claimed. It was black and ugly, like any aircraft carrier at night. The chopper landed as soft as a feather, and after a few minutes I was led to the captain's quarters where I hoped to find Hawk.

I found the captain, as grim a man as his Cobra pilot-killer.

"There was an explosion in a toy factory in Hiroshima," he said, motioning me to a chair and puffing on a black cigar that I could have sworn had been given to him by David Hawk. "The factory is coming out with a secret new toy robot for the Christmas rush and your people in Washington think perhaps an American competitor might be to blame for the explosion. Your job is to get to the bottom of things before an anti-American campaign begins in Japan. You're to contact a man named Tumio when you reach Tokyo. Instructions and your contact's phone number and address are here." He shoved a Manila envelope across the desk. "The owner of the factory is Nashima Porfiro, a friend of your boss. Any questions?"

"A toy factory?"

The captain nodded, grimly. He seemed to get some satisfaction out of my incredulity. He suspected that I was some kind of crackerjack agent, though he couldn't know anything about AXE, the most supersecret espionage organization extant in America. The captain probably didn't even know Hawk's brand of nauseating cigars.

"That's all there is to the orders?" I asked. "Just check out an explosion in a toy factory that's turning out toy robots for the Christmas rush?"

"That's it, Mr. Carter," he said, his lips smiling

just a bit. "I don't suppose I have to explain to you the touchiness of the situation. If an American competitor set off that explosion, he couldn't have picked a worse place for it. Any place but Hiroshima. Or perhaps Nagasaki. Because of what happened at the end of World War Two, both cities are hotbeds of anti-American feeling. Your job might not be as easy as you think, or as frivolous."

I thought about it. Yes, those were the only two cities in the world to have suffered the disastrous effects of atomic bombs. And Americans had dropped those bombs, in a successful effort to end the war and save the lives of countless millions of soldiers on both sides. But a toy factory? I saw no frying-pan-to-fire in that.

"We have an F-14 all prepped to fly you to San Francisco," the captain said. "There, you'll board a commercial flight to Tokyo. Your tickets, money and credentials are here." He shoved yet another manila envelope at me.

"A toy factory," I muttered.

"A toy factory," he echoed. "Christmas toys. Robots." Then, he smiled openly. "Good luck. I hear you'll probably need it."

TWO

The Pan Am 747 dropped through clouds toward Tokyo International just as I lit up the thirtieth of my special Turkish blend, gold-tipped cigarettes with my initials on the filter. I'd stocked up in San Francisco just before calling Hawk to find out more about this lousy toy factory.

He'd been mad as hell that I'd called. And he hadn't been much help.

He hinted of terrorists in Japan and I found that hard to believe. At least not anti-American terrorists. He admitted that my new assignment was partly to help someone he'd befriended in 1945 when he had been stationed in Japan as part of the Occupation Force.

"It may turn out to be something big," Hawk had said. "Just play it by ear and don't underestimate anything or anyone. Don't call unless you're in absolutely desperate straits. And don't let down my friend, Nashima."

So, here I was, just hours after nearly being wiped out on a sandy ledge above a Colombian beach, on my way to save a toy factory in Japan.

The only pleasant part of the assignment so far was a stewardess named Pira. Young, shapely and as cute as an ant's antenna, she had been especially attentive to the "toy salesman" named Peter Holmes. That was me, per the credentials given me by the captain of the *Constellation*. Once again, I was on my own, without portfolio, without backup.

Pira came by, smiled, kept on going. I winked and nodded for her to return when she got the chance. Two minutes later, she was sitting on the arm of the seat, her perfectly shaped behind touching my upper arm. I flexed my muscles to let her know that I was aware of that nice touch.

"You need something else, Mister Homes?" Pira asked, leaving out the L. Her dark, slanted eyes twinkled. Her thin, red lips smiled with mischief. Her small breasts moved sensually beneath her tight Pan Am blouse.

"Just one thing," I said. "I'm a man of a few words. I have tonight free in Tokyo and I'd like us to do something really expensive together."

The smile didn't miss a beat. "I thought you'd never ask," she said. "This is my last journey, so I don't have to abide by company rules about dating passengers. We can even disembark together."

"You're quitting flying?"

"Yes. I've saved enough to finish my studies. I have two years to go."

"Studying what?"

"Nuclear physics."

"You're kidding." All those looks and brains too?"

"I'm a woman of a few words, Mr. Homes," she said, those dark eyes twinkling with new mischief. "I don't kid."

She got up and went forward. The FASTEN SEAT BELT sign came on, and I fastened mine by rote, waiting for the plane to land. I didn't see Pira until the plane was taxiing up to the big motorized tube that snags onto the side of the plane like the mouth of a leech.

She was waiting up front, beside another stewardess and the flight steward.

I picked up my briefcase of toy catalogues, left for me in a locker at the airport in San Francisco, and joined the stream of passengers in the aisle. At the door, Pira said a final goodbye to her former co-workers, smiled sweetly up at me and took my arm. We followed a young mother and her small child out the door and into the tube.

Pira was laughing gaily and asking me about our dinner plans as we entered the airport. I was just opening my mouth to tell her the name of a place recommended to me when I heard the sharp reports from across the concourse.

Three men, who'd hastily pulled black hoods over their heads, stood like robots, feet planted apart, immense automatic rifles gripped in their hands.

An execution squad.

"Hit the deck," I yelled to Pira as the young mother in front of us fell from a gunshot to the chest. Her baby, possibly a year old, tumbled from her arms, unhurt, and began to scream hysterically.

I grabbed Pira on my way down. Her body didn't resist. In fact, it dropped under my hand like a sack of warm water. For the moment, I didn't have time to worry about that. The copper and steel bullets from the three automatic weapons were zeroing in on me.

The pandemonium of passengers and visitors in the concourse no doubt saved my life. People screamed and ran in every conceivable direction. A whole flock of them passed between me and the three gunmen.

I had no weapons, so I was in no mood or condition for heroics. I lay flat against the carpet, my arm covering and holding down an unresisting Pira.

In that moment, I had a sick premonition about the girl, but had no time to confirm it. I hugged the carpet, listened to the shrieks and yells, the pounding of footsteps. Suddenly, I realized that there were no more gunshots.

I raised my head, strained to see through the milling crowd. Sure enough, the spot across the concourse where the three men had stood firing their weapons was empty.

Policemen in uniform were dashing everywhere, pushing people aside, converging on that spot.

A part of my mind wanted to believe that some hotheaded terrorists had merely left a bloody calling card by shooting into a crowd of innocent airline passengers from San Francisco.

But I knew better.

That execution squad had been sent to kill me. I was no longer Peter Holmes, toy salesman.

I was Nick Carter, N3, Killmaster for AXE.

I was a target.

The executioners had missed their prime target. I felt good about that. I felt bad about the young mother in front of me, who had taken a bullet meant for me. She was dead, gushing blood. Her child was clinging to her, crying.

And then my premonition about Pira proved true.

She was limp beside me. I rose to my knees and turned her over. Behind us, other passengers were rising. One of them screamed when she saw the holes in Pira's chest.

Three bullet holes, each marked by a crimson circle of blood.

Pira's eyes were closed. Her face slack in death. On the floor where she had lain was a large patch of blood.

I felt vomit rising in my throat, when a policeman barged up beside us.

"You know this girl?" he demanded.

"Her name is Pira," I said, without thinking. "She was a stewardess on the flight that just came in. I—"

"Move back," the policeman said to a group of curious passengers who'd moved in to peer at Pira's body.

I took that opportunity to get the hell out of there.

Snipers were waiting. An execution squad was waiting. I couldn't get involved in any official inquiries.

Newsmen would be on the scene soon. Television and still cameras. Behind any of those cameras could loom an automatic rifle.

I ran like the wind, leaping the counter at Customs, leaving my luggage behind.

Leaving beautiful Pira behind.

Leaving a screaming, heartbroken child behind.

Carrying a new respect for my assignment to cover an explosion in a toy factory.

THREE

The speedy, sophisticated and thoroughly modern monorail that linked the airport with the downtown section, or Chiyoda-ku, of Tokyo rumbled along softly. It was only a bit crowded. Taking public transportation bought me some time, I felt, for the killers would expect a spy, or a hot-shot American toy salesman, to take a limo or taxi.

According to the data in my manila envelope, Tumio lived in Arakawa-ku, in the northern part of the city. His address, 47713 Kototoi-dori, was just north of Ueno Park and Zoo, east of Tokyo University.

I got off the monorail on Showa-dori, one block down from Ginza Street, walked up to Ginza and farther north to the Imperial Hotel. I had rooms reserved at the Imperial, a gaudy but splendid structure designed by Frank Lloyd Wright.

Near the hotel, I took a taxi, rode it as far as Kasuga-dori, got off and took a public bus to Shinobazu-dori. From there, I walked down toward Ueno Park, past the Tokyo Gallery of Fine

Arts, then reversed my steps past the Tokyo National Museum and National Science Museum, strolled through the zoo and came out on Kototoi-dori, a broad east-west avenue filled with modern apartment buildings of the fast-rising upper middle class.

I staked out Tumio's building for an hour, until darkness was upon the city, saw nothing of import or danger. Even so, I was taking no chances on meeting those black-hooded three stooges with their automatic weapons. I could still see those crimson circles on Pira's lovely chest.

From a drugstore at the corner, right next to a stall that sold live, plucked chickens, I called Tumio's apartment.

"Ohio," he said when he picked up the receiver.

Tumio had become westernized, but only to a certain point. His greeting was the Japanese word for "hello."

"Michigan," I came back at him. "Go Blue."

My code response had to do with the annual football rivalry between Ohio State and Michigan. "Go Blue" was Michigan's battle cry.

"What you really mean," Tumio said with a chuckle, "is go to hell, Blue.' Right?"

He'd given the correct answer, the one that told me he was in no danger, not under duress from nearby threatening guns.

"Right," I said. "Mix up some martinis. I'll be right up."

Tumio was a small, genial, eternally smiling young man. At thirty-nine, he was already a vice president of the Porfiro Toy Company of Hiroshima.

"Since our rendezvous was scheduled for tomorrow," Tumio said, smiling and pouring me a martini, straight up, "I must assume that you ran into difficulty."

I told him about the execution squad at the airport. He smiled and nodded, as though I were discussing the latest baseball standings in which his team placed on top.

"Do you know who those guys are?" I asked, beginning to suspect that this whole thing was some kind of crummy joke.

"Yes, but I think it best that Nashima Porfiro, my employer in Hiroshima, fill in the details. Will you stay on schedule with your visit there, or will you go tonight?"

"Is there a plane leaving tonight?"

"Several, but they'll be watching them. The Tokaido leaves in one hour."

The Tokaido is the world's fastest train—until the one in France is completed. I hadn't been on it in years.

"I'll be on the Tokaido," I said. "Now, about those goons at the airport. I want—"

"My employer," he repeated, smiling again and pouring me another drink, "has insisted that all details be reserved for your arrival in Hiroshima. I am to provide you with weapons and any directions you might need. And, of course, sanctuary if you should be in danger."

I was getting a bit pissed.

"This is all pretty damned hush-hush and gory just because a bunch of American toymakers are trying to steal or sabotage your employer's latest gadget. What the hell is really going down, Tumio?"

He smiled. "More martini?"

"Okay, I get the message. Your employer wants to hog all the details for himself. But what makes you think those goons won't be expecting me on the Tokaido?"

"Simple," he said, handing me the telephone. "Call and make a reservation on Nippon Airways Flight 51. One of the Sons will most assuredly learn of the reservation and—"

"Sons?"

He smiled, but there was nervousness in it now. "My employer in Hiroshima . . ."

"Will fill me in on the details. Thanks for the martinis, Tumio. Now, give me my weapons and I'll be off."

Predictably, the weapons were in a manila envelope. Wilhelmina, my favorite handgun, plus six spare clips of 9mm Luger slugs. Hugo, a nasty, six-inch-blade stiletto in a sheath designed to be carried on the forearm. And Pierre, the lethal little gas bomb that I normally carry in a sheepskin pouch as a third testicle on my right thigh.

The weapons were one more reason why I would have to take the train and not a plane. They don't check you on trains. Even if I hadn't lost Wilhelmina on that ledge above the Pacific Ocean, I would have arrived in Tokyo empty-handed.

Hawk was not about to push for special dispensation for a toy salesman named Peter Holmes.

"Goodbye, Mr. Holmes," Tumio said, pronouncing the L with emphasis and opening the door for me.

"If you should have further need of me, you have my number here and at the office. I would prefer that you call me here. There are Sons at the Tokyo office as well."

There it was again. Sons. *Who the hell were the Sons?*

FOUR

The train didn't seem to be going fast, but it was. We reached a hundred and eighty not more than ten miles out of Tokyo. The 425-mile trip to Hiroshima in the southwestern part of the country would take less than three hours.

There were several lovely stewardesses on the sleek, ultra-comfortable train. Four of them had all the charm of the girl named Pira. I studiously avoided making friends with any of them, recalling those horrible moments when Pira and I had emerged from that tube into Tokyo International Airport.

There could be a repeat of the execution squad when the Tokaido reached Hiroshima, but I'd brook no repeat of Pira. And, when the train arrived, I'd make sure to separate myself from the other passengers.

I slept a bit, cursed Tumio for being such a stickler for protocol, dreamed about all the Piras of the world and was shocked when the trainmaster announced arrival in Hiroshima Central Station just two hours and twenty-eight minutes after the train had left Tokyo.

I had made two reservations when I'd been in Tumio's apartment. One for a plane that I had no intentions of taking. A second for a room at the Shiko-Plaza, not far from Peace Park and the Peace Memorial—site of a shrine in memory of the thousands killed in the atomic bomb blast of August 6, 1945. I thought about walking up to the park to see the memorial, the bell tower and the enormous ruined building left as a reminder, but I had to know what was waiting for me at the hotel.

As yet, I hesitated to rent a car. I'd have to use the phony driver's license issued to Peter Holmes, and the Sons were looking for Peter Holmes.

I signed the register and watched the face of the clerk as he read my signature, then booked me in Room 911. Nothing there. No sign that he recognized the name or attached any significance to it.

So far, so good.

Yet, an old spy's sense of danger was vacillating deep inside me, fluttering around like a newly molted butterfly. As I waited for the elevator, I remembered a night in Washington when I'd tried to outsmart a Soviet spy and he had waited for me to come down on the elevator. He'd been waiting there when the doors slid open, and he'd nearly blown me to hell and back.

As an exercise, I strolled away from the elevator doors and pretended to read a poster. It was in Japanese, showing a lovely girl, who looked a great deal like Pira, at a microphone. I figured it was a sign announcing the entertainment in the hotel lounge.

The doors opened. I turned slowly, expecting to see three men with black hoods and automatic rifles.

The elevator was empty. I stepped aboard, pushed number nine, waited until the elevator reached the third floor, then pushed number seven. I got off there and walked up two flights.

Room 911 was halfway down the corridor, equidistant from the elevator and the staircase. Bad location. I should have insisted on a room near an exit, but I hadn't wanted to draw any more attention to myself than necessary.

At the door, I got out the key, recalling how disappointed the bell captain had been when I arrived without luggage. He couldn't assign a bellhop, share in the tip. So, I'd given the guy a thousand yen—about five dollars—to salve his disappointment. Who could tell when I might need his services in other areas?

The thousand yen paid off. Just as I was starting to insert the key, the elevator doors opened and the bell captain came running toward me. I steeled myself, my hand on Wilhelmina under my left armpit.

"Mr. Homes-san," the bell captain said, leaving out the L. "I meant to tell you that you had company earlier. Two men came to ask about you. The clerk said you would arrive later and that he would assign you room 911."

"Did you see the men come upstairs?"

"No, Mr. Homes-san. But then I was diverted by another guest requiring assistance. Were you expecting friends to call?"

I shook my head, unwilling to make any more sounds in that corridor. That spy sense of danger was positively rattling around in my psyche now. I put my finger to my lips in the universal gesture for silence, gave the bell captain another thousand yen and motioned him away. He went quietly and I stood facing the door, wondering who was behind it, and why.

All right. I could play their game. I was about to kick in the door, with Wilhelmina in one hand and Hugo in the other, but decided against it.

Maybe nobody was in Room 911. Maybe they'd come and left.

Maybe they'd planted a calling card for me.

There were many ways to find out. The best was to call the bell captain back and let him open the door, let him earn his two thousand yen in a big way. Or, I could have called the authorities, suggested they open the door.

Again, each way would draw more attention to me.

There was a third way. My way.

I turned to Room 912, directly across the corridor. I knocked, gently. No answer. I checked the locking mechanism and saw that a plastic credit card would do the job nicely.

A minute later, I was inside the room. It was occupied, from the looks of clothing and suitcases strewn around the place, but the occupants were gone.

I went to the far end of the room, near the window. I pulled a heavy armchair in front of me and knelt behind it. I laid Wilhelmina on top of the chair and aimed through the open door. I aimed for the keyhole of Room 911.

The boom of the Luger was still ringing in my ears when I heard a second explosion, saw a ball of flame and debris fly into the corridor from Room 911.

The concussion reached the chair and me within a fraction of a second. The heavy chair was blown back against me, knocking me into the wall just below the window.

If I'd been standing, I'd have been shredded, then blown out the window.

As it was, the chair and the whole room were on fire. The corridor beyond the open door was a roaring inferno.

They'd left a calling card, all right. I guessed it at about ten pounds of TNT.

I heard shouts from down the corridor, heard the crackling flames. I checked the window behind me, saw a small patio. I opened the window and stepped out, shinnying down to the next patio. There, I broke a window in a darkened room, walked past a young couple making love, stepped into the corridor and walked all the way down to the lobby.

From the lounge came the sweet strains of a Japanese girl crooning American love songs. From the street came the sounds of sirens.

It was time to check into another hotel, then pay a call on Nashima Porfiro.

FIVE

The Porfiro residence was in Marika-ku, one of the oldest, most traditional and most beautiful parts of Hiroshima. I'd done a bit of homework on the A-bomb city and learned that it had fame before the coming of the atomic age.

Built in 1594 as a fortress against marauding Chinese, the lovely city lies on six small islands in the Ota River, not far from the Sea of Japan. Eighty bridges link the various parts of the bustling city of more than six hundred thousand.

I had the taxi driver cruise up and down Namura-dori for twenty minutes, passing stacks of yen over the back of the seat to keep him from getting edgy. I still wasn't in the mood to rent a car until I learned more about the mysterious Sons and how they knew who I was and why I was here.

"Okay, stop here and let me out." I paid him off.

"Long wok back to city," he said. "Not want me to wait?"

"No, thanks. It's a nice night for a walk," I said, grinning.

To make certain he didn't know my real destination, I'd pretended to admire all the great walled mansions along Namura-dori. And I had him let me out a half-mile from the Porfiro residence, then had walked off into the darkness the other way. Once he was gone, and I was sure of it, I circled around to Nashima Porfiro's place and climbed the wall at one side.

It was quiet, and I admired the lovely gardens in the distance, beyond well-tailored lawns. Small buildings, pagodas, loomed against the sky that was not very dark for the lateness of the night. A stream ran beneath colorful, ornate bridges. I ignored the bridges and jumped the stream when I needed to get closer to the main part of the immense compound of buildings.

After checking out the property and finding it clean, I went to the front door and pulled a chain that I presumed was some kind of doorbell. Chimes somewhere inside played a lovely six-note melody.

The door opened and I was staring, open-mouthed, at the most beautiful woman I have ever seen. She appeared to be middle-aged and was quite tall for a Japanese. An ornately embroidered silk kimono adorned her stunning body, while all manner of expensive jewelry blazed from wrists, neck and ears. There was even a striking jade embedded in the tight hairdo, just above her forehead.

"Konichi-wa," she said in greeting, smiling with impish glee at my dumbfounded expression. "Won't you please come in, Mr. Holmes?" She pronounced the L exquisitely.

She backed away from the door with a slight bow. When her head dipped, light from inside caught the jade and made it blaze in my eyes. I hesitated, wondering if perhaps I might be entering another trap. She was one lovely lady spider enticing the fly like that.

"Don't be shy, Mr. Holmes," the woman said. "David said you had no shy bones in your body. But then, his description of you really doesn't do justice to your handsomeness."

"I came to see Mr. Porfiro," I stammered as I went in. The house was an extension of the lady's perfection—mostly Japanese motif with shoji screens and silk tapestries and low tables with cushions instead of chairs. There were also Western-style chairs and tables, and two Renoirs, sticking out like flaring rockets beside Japanese-style paintings of some imposing, snow-capped mountain. "Is he here?"

She shook her head and closed the door. As she folded her slender hands in front of her, the folds of the kimono revealed ample breasts that were high and enticing.

"There is no Mr. Porfiro," she said. "Not anymore. My husband died ten years ago. I am Nashima Porfiro."

No way, I figured. Nashima Porfiro might not be a man, but Nashima Porfiro couldn't possibly be such a beautiful young-looking woman.

"I think you'd better explain," I said, looking around to see if some black-hooded goons might come snaking out from behind a shoji screen.

She shrugged and let the folds of silk fall back in place. She preceded me into the living room and motioned me to a Western-style armchair.

"There is nothing to explain. Did not David Hawk tell you that I was a woman?"

"For starters," I said, sitting in the chair but not relaxing in it, "I expected someone closer to Hawk's age. After all, you two are supposed to be friends dating back to 1945. I'd guess that you were no more than a gleam in some returning warrior's eye in 1945."

"I was thirteen," she said. "Now, I am closer to fifty, one side or the other."

Impossible. Yet, there was a calm maturity around her eyes and mouth. No wrinkles, but hints of them. But her skin was so flawless, so translucent. And those high, full breasts. Plastic surgery? Possibly.

"Maybe you'd better tell me about you and David Hawk," I said, lighting up a cigarette. "After that, I want a full update on what's happening here and why David Hawk asked me to come see you."

She sat in a second armchair, crossed perfectly-shaped legs and lit up a long, slender cigarette. She told me things I hadn't even dreamed about my boss.

"David was a lieutenant in Army Intelligence," she said. "Part of the Army of Occupation. My father, Oji Anjino, had been listed as missing in action in 1944. My mother had no money to keep the family together, so she sold me to a geisha master and my baby brothers were put out for adoption."

"And you were only twelve?"

She smiled, ruefully, hardly missing an old custom that had brought misfortune and unhappiness to a country's womenfolk. And childfolk.

"Some were sold at ten. I was much more seasoned. I met Lieutenant David Hawk a year later, when he came to our place of business. There were three of us geishas attending him. When he learned that I was only thirteen, he was outraged. I could not comprehend why he was angry. Now, I know."

"And that's the extent of your friendship?" I said.

"Hardly. Our David Hawk is not to be underestimated. He bought me from the geisha master and enrolled me in school. I had thought that he would return for me, since I then belonged to him, but he merely visited me at the school several times, bringing gifts suitable for girls of thirteen. It was clear that he did not think of me as an object of sex. By the time he had to leave Japan, at the end of his tour of duty, I was hopelessly in love with him. And he with me."

"In love?" It didn't seem to fit Hawk.

"Yes, but not the way you think. I loved him as a man and longed to be his wife. He loved me as a daughter and longed to bring me to America. He was then engaged and planned to marry. He wanted to adopt me."

Yeah, that sounded like Hawk.

"It was impossible, for a variety of reasons," she said, again with the rueful smile. "Three years after the war, Lieutenant David Hawk found my father in a hospital in Manila. He had been wounded and had amnesia. David paid for his recovery. You see, our country was in great economic turmoil then. The Government could not afford to take care of its returning warriors. Not adequately, anyway. My job thus was to stay with my father, nurse him, take care of him."

"While still going to school?"

"Yes. I studied business at Tokyo University. There, I met Najita Porfiro, a brilliant young man with no money. By the time we had finished our studies, my father had recovered his memory. One of his first and perhaps most important memories was the fact that, before the war, he had hidden a great cache of gold."

"If your mother had known that," I said, "she wouldn't have had to sell you into the geisha houses."

"Yes, she would," Nashima responded. "The Government would have taken the gold and given nothing in return. For the war effort, you see. That's why my father hid the gold in the first place.

"Najita Porfiro and I were married in 1952, the same year my father bought one of the oldest toy companies in Japan. My father headed the company until he became incapacitated and then my husband headed it, changing its name from the Anjino Toy Company to the Porfiro Toy Company. When my husband died ten years ago, I was finally able to use the education that David Hawk had paid for. I became the head of the company."

"And your baby brothers? Were they found? And where is your mother now?"

"One brother was found," she said, averting her gaze from my eyes. I sensed that she was skirting the truth now, but had no idea why. "My brother is not well, as you will see. As for my mother, she took her own life on the day the war ended." She raised her eyes to mine again, shook off her sad thoughts and said brightly, "Tell me, Mr. Holmes, when you first saw me at the door, how old did you think I was?"

I decided not to feed her ego. I countered with a question. "You tell me, Mrs. Porfiro, how come you weren't surprised to see me tonight? I'm not due here until tomorrow."

"Tumio called from Tokyo," she said. "He told me everything."

"All right," I said. "So we have part of the story. Your old friendship with Hawk is understandable. Why did you call him for help?"

She folded the slender hands across her knees, sighed deeply. "It was a difficult decision," she said. "David Hawk visited me three years ago. He said he was in the export business, but I didn't believe him. I know him too well, and sensed he had something to do with the government. A powerful man. Since Americans are being blamed for the explosion at my factory, I thought he should know. Pardon me for saying this, but I had hoped that David would come himself."

"I like honesty," I said. "I hope I don't prove too disappointing."

"It was unkind of me to say that," she said, "but you must know that I still love David Hawk. I always shall. Now, let me tell you what has happened and what I think it means."

She told of how one of the factory's engineers had designed a sophisticated robot that could perform like a computer, do menial tasks, climb stairs, talk, answer difficult questions—in short, be much more than a toy to any child. It could be a playmate, a teacher, a mechanical slave. During her explanation, I got the feeling that she was choosing her words well, even leaving things out. I had a zillion questions when she finished.

"First off, how much does this marvel cost?"

"We haven't established cost yet." A dark cloud seemed to pass behind her lovely black eyes and I knew she was lying, or evading. "But it will not be too expensive."

"And the idea is that some American toy manufacturer, trying to steal the secret or to put a monkey wrench into the works, set off an explosion in your factory?"

Again the dark cloud. "That is the opinion of our manager, Nato Nakuma. He tells everyone that. I am afraid that, if the word spreads too widely, animosity against Americans will grow, spread to the automobile industry where there is already animosity. We're quite sensitive to the problems of the American auto industry, the fact that such problems are blamed on Japanese exports. Or imports, depending on where you are."

I didn't buy that. If this were a simple case of industrial spies trying to steal secrets or to disrupt competitors, it was nothing new. There was no reason to expect it to spread to greater violence or to other industries. Nashima, for all her great beauty, charm and brains, was either holding something back, or she was looking at the situation cockeyed.

"Where does this Nato Nakuma get his information?" I asked. "Does he know for certain that Americans are involved? It could be another Japanese toymaker, you know."

"No," she said quickly. "No, I can only go on what our factory manager says. He is a very trustworthy man, very honorable."

Yeah. Honorable. Another old custom that had about as much worth as the geisha system. Except we all knew what the geishas were doing. We couldn't trust the honorable ones any further than we could throw them.

"Tell me, Nashima," I said, watching her growing nervousness, "what do you know about an organization called the Sons?"

Her chalk white skin went even whiter. Her hands fluttered in her lap. Her head bowed until the jade was sending laser beams of light all through the room.

"My God," she said, surprising me. "I should have known it would be a mistake to call on David Hawk. I am always underestimating him."

"And what is that supposed to mean?"

"It means," she said, looking up at me with tears in her lovely eyes, "that I have signed my death warrant by calling David Hawk. You, Mr. Holmes—otherwise known as Nick Carter—are to be the instrument of my death."

SIX

The lady had been holding back, all right. But not in the way I had suspected.

She told me about the Sons.

They were a terrorist group that operated for the moment in only two Japanese cities: Hiroshima and Nagasaki. Their purpose was to wreak havoc on Americans in Japan, including all American-owned/operated/controlled companies.

They called themselves the Sons of August Six.

Their vendetta against Americans was their way of paying America back for the dropping of the first atomic bomb on August 6, 1945.

I expressed amazement to Nashima Porfiro that David Hawk hadn't known about this group.

"That is easy to explain," she said, wringing her hands in anguish now. "The Sons work in secrecy. Many of their terrorist attacks are blamed on others, or on accidents. Or, as in the case with my factory, on American competitors. And there is something else."

"What is it?"

"They use threats on Japanese people who know of them. Insidious threats. If they were to know that I was talking to you, that I had called David Hawk, they would not only eliminate me, they would kill every member of my family, including distant cousins—relatives I've never even seen."

"I see. Do you think the Sons of August Six had anything to do with the explosion at your factory?"

The dark clouds passed behind those eyes. She was getting ready to evade again, possibly even lie.

"Nato Nakuma says it is impossible. He says the Americans did it. He found bits of explosive devices in the factory that were made in America."

I wouldn't let her off the hook that easily. "I don't give a damn what Nato Nakuma thinks or says. Tell me what you think."

She bowed her head; tears dropped to the silk kimono. I felt sorry for her, because I knew the answer.

Nashima Porfiro, this beautiful woman with the youthful face and desirable body, had been threatened by the Sons of August Six. An insidious threat.

"Have you told the police that you've been threatened?" I asked.

She turned white again. "Who said I was threatened?"

I shook my head, sadly. She wouldn't tell me what I needed to know. I took a different tack.

"What do the police think happened at the factory, about who set off the explosion?"

"The police weren't called," she said.

Her answer startled me. "Why the hell not?"

She smiled, not very convincingly. "It is practice among companies here to keep such things to themselves. Nato thought it best not to bring them in on it. If it is industrial espionage, he and his people will handle it, he says. As for telling the police that I'd been threatened by the Sons of August—if such a threat had been made—you must understand that the police are heavily infiltrated by the Sons of August Six. It would have been useless. But I haven't been threatened, Nick. You must believe it."

"Okay, I won't push you on that. But I do have a question you have to answer, threat or not."

She looked up. "Yes? What is the question?"

"Who did you tell about your call to David Hawk? Who knew that I was coming here under the name of Peter Holmes, toy salesman?"

"I told no one. I took it upon myself to call David. I even registered in the Shiko-Plaza under an assumed name. I made the call from there."

The Shiko-Plaza. I remembered it well, remembered how Room 911 blew all to hell with one quick punch from Wilhelmina.

"Someone knew," I told her. "You're certain you didn't tell your factory manager, Nakuma?"

"I told no one." She said it with emphasis, pressing her thin lips together in a crimson line. I looked away from the color.

"Your secretary. You do have a secretary, don't

you? Did you tell her? Or him?"

—"Nato and I share a secretary. Her name is Kiko Shoshoni. She's very young, but she's been with the company since she was sixteen. We trained her. But I told her nothing of my plan to call David."

"How about Tumio?" I said. "The company's vice president in Tokyo. You had to tell him something and you gave Hawk his number to contact so that he could provide weapons for me. How much does he know?"

Her face went red, not white. It was the red of rage. "You are not to suspect Tumio," she blurted. "He is our most trusted employee. He knows little. And he certainly would not betray me. There . . . there are reasons."

I figured Tumio to be a lover and let it go at that. Except I was a bit jealous. "And you made the hotel reservations at the Shiko-Plaza all by yourself. You didn't trust it to Kiko, or to your father or brother?"

"I live in this house with my father who is recovering from another stroke," she said, her eyes sad and listless. "As for my brother, I told you he was not well. He is—How do you say it in America?—retarded."

"Are they under the same threat as you are?"

Her head bolted upright. Her eyes, no longer filled with tears or rage, were now filled with fright.

"Who said I was threatened?"

"You did, in effect. You said you'd signed your

death warrant by calling Hawk. You even said I was to be the instrument of your death."

She smiled, again not very convincingly. "Isn't it obvious that the Sons of August Six know about you? They tried to kill you twice. If they know of you, they certainly must know that you were summoned. If they do not now know that I was the one who sent for you, they will find out. That is all I meant."

"And how are they going to find out?"

"They might take you alive, make you talk."

"Lady, I've been worked on by experts, even the Chinese."

Her smile was chilling. "The Chinese have the reputation for being experts in torture to make victims talk, but the Japanese are far more cruel, far more effective."

"I'll take my chances." I stood up. I'd learned all I was going to learn from this beautiful lady. As much as I wanted to stay, hoping she'd even admit me as a house guest, she was too shaken up to play the perfect hostess. "See you tomorrow at the factory. We might as well keep up the ruse and pretend that I'm a toy salesman. I'd like to see what I can find there, talk to Nato and Kiko."

She appeared fearful again, as though she wanted to back down on her request for help.

"Don't worry," I said. "I'll be discreet. Meanwhile, don't tell anyone—not even your father or your brother—who I really am."

That made her hot again. Her dark eyes flared

with anger. "I trust my father and brother implicitly," she snapped.

"So do I, Nashima," I said, gently, sorry I'd offended her. "But, as you said, the Chinese have the reputation, the Japanese have the cruelty, the effectiveness. I don't want any of those Sons coming around asking your father or your brother questions."

Her smile was almost genuine. "I see. Please forgive me for not understanding."

"Forgiven."

I got the hell out of there before I started begging to be admitted as a house guest.

SEVEN

The Porfiro Toy Factory lay on the southern-most island of the group of six that makes up Hiroshima. It was big, sprawling, the main section three stories high. There were separate buildings, including a huge, one-story warehouse. The end of one wing, near a loading dock, showed signs of the explosion that had torn it to pieces. The enterprising workers had rigged a shed leading to the dock and other workers were already taking the ruined section apart for rebuilding.

The whole thing was surrounded by a high chainlink fence with barbed wire at the top, concentration camp-style. Every window in the place had heavy steel bars covering it.

Nashima hadn't arrived. Still following an old custom, she would reach her office shortly before noon, work until two o'clock, take a lengthy tea and then work until seven or eight.

But Kiko Shoshoni was there, bright and cheerful and as helpful and adorable as a trained puppy.

"Oh, Mister Holmes-san, so happy making your acquaintance. Lady Porfiro has told me so much about you. I have the honor all to myself of showing you around the factory."

I followed her from the lobby and away from the intense glare of the Sumo wrestler-sized receptionist who had grudgingly called Kiko to come fetch me. Kiko was such a pleasant counterpart. Slim, yet well-endowed of hips and breasts, she had long black hair, divinely-shaped almond eyes, clear, translucent skin and a soft, melodic voice. The young woman clearly radiated sex, yet I found that, in all that lust, the major portion of it was reserved for the lovely lady named Nashima.

We were halfway through the factory tour before I took my eyes off Kiko's well-rounded buttocks and full breasts enough to see that the workers, who were assembling various parts of a really classy toy robot, were glaring at me with equal parts of suspicion, fear and hatred.

What the hell, I was only a humble toy salesman from America, come to look over the wares I'd soon be selling to department store buyers all over the States. I was, ostensibly, here to help these people make a living, keep their jobs, make more and more robot toys so that American children could know the true joy of playing with a most superior toy.

There was little to see in the section that had suffered the brunt of the explosion. Workers had cleared away virtually all the shattered and burned debris. There was the smell of cordite hanging all about the explosion site, though. Some really powerful stuff had been planted here—as it had against the inside of the door to Room 911 in the Shiko-Plaza.

Kiko led me to the little makeshift shed where the finished toy robots were being packed for shipping.

"This shipping place is only one of several, Mister Holmes," she explained. "Toys from this area go to such places as Australia and Germany. Toys going to America are sent through the next wing over there."

I looked at the row of tiny robots lined up on a newly installed conveyor belt. Each robot was eighteen inches high and looked suspiciously like Artoo-Deetoo from *Star Wars*. I didn't get to see the robots perform, but I wanted a closer look. I reached out to pick one up and Kiko tugged at my arm.

"Let me show you the designers' room," she said, pulling me away from the conveyor belt. "I'd like to introduce you to the man who conceived these robots."

I met the engineer, a little guy with inch-thick glasses. A great toy designer, but a lousy conversationalist, I got no information from him.

"I think you've seen enough of the factory for today," Kiko said when we left the engineer. "Lady Porfiro gave me explicit instructions to show you some sights, too. Come on, you can drive."

She had a small battered Buick, a disappointment since I'd looked forward to driving a Toyota on its home grounds. Her directions to the city were no better than her driving.

After we'd crossed and recrossed one bridge four times, I decided to go homing pigeon style and soon found the downtown section all by myself.

I was about to ask her why she hadn't wanted me to pick up that toy robot, and why she hadn't introduced me to Nato Nakuma, the factory manager, when she grabbed the wheel and yanked hard to the right. We were in the middle of a block.

"Turn left," she piped.

"We go straight," I said, righting the wheel to keep from crashing the Buick into a fish stand. "If you don't mind, I'd like to follow the streets the way they were laid out."

"Beg your pardon?"

"Never mind. Where is it you want to take me?"

"To Peace Park. Where were you the day the bomb was dropped?"

Most people in the world can tell you to the minute what they did that day. As for me, I had no idea where I was on perhaps the most important day in the history of the world—the dawning of the atomic age. An age that some think will be our last, as a result of our having entered it.

"I don't know, Kiko," I said honestly.

Her incredible chatter kept up as we toured the Peace Park and Peace Memorial Hall. We weren't allowed in the huge building that had been left as a memorial to the blast itself. Fortunately, I'd done my homework on the place; Kiko didn't have much to tell me.

"And now," she said as we stood before the memorial arch and I read the lengthy inscription, "let's go back to my apartment." There was a twinkle in her eyes.

"More orders from Mrs. Porfiro?" I asked.

"No," she said, squeezing my arm as we walked hip to hip back to the battered little Buick. "This is my idea. You like?"

"I'll let you know."

Her apartment was small, but well-appointed and comfortable. She lived only a few blocks from the downtown section in a new, modern, but rather cheaply built area for the lower middle class.

But I paid little attention to her living quarters.

We were no sooner inside than Kiko, who'd contented herself with little squeezes and hip-rubbings in public, turned and slid into my arms with a vehemence that jolted me. She rammed her hips hard into mine and began to gyrate her mound against my thickening penis.

As soon as she felt the full hardness, she slid down my frame, her hands caressing me through my clothing. She unzipped my trousers, took out the aroused member and moved her breasts up and down against it.

There was a lot of the geisha in this girl, who seemed to know virtually all there was about the pleasures of sex, about how to make a man appreciate her body—and his—during the act of love.

Without becoming too clinical in my description

of her love-making, let's just say the greater part of it consisted of Kiko thoroughly examining, caressing, kissing and adoring my entire body as though each part was a precious gem.

After more than two hours of exquisite pleasure, we decided to get something to eat. The restaurant Kiko chose was a scrumptious seafood place beneath one of the eighty bridges. We'd both worked up hearty appetites, and ate ravenously, though Kiko chattered animatedly during the entire meal.

The only shadow on an otherwise perfect evening was the fact that I still had dangerous work to do, and little knowledge of how to do it and still survive.

No. There was a second shadow.

I kept wishing Kiko Shoshoni was Nashima Porfiro.

In spite of Kiko's insistence that I stay the night in her apartment, I dropped her off around midnight and headed back to the hotel. On foot.

A block from the hotel, I heard the explosion. It was muffled by distance, but I recognized the tone and timbre of that explosion.

Another hotel room had disappeared in a fiery halo of TNT. I wondered who had triggered it.

I went back to Kiko's apartment where she greeted me with a broadside of chatter and of good things to come, but I went straight to her television set and turned it on. Orson Welles was in the middle of a long monologue—with Japanese subtitles—from *Citizen Kane*. I sat on a pillow with Kiko gently rubbing my neck and shoulders, and waited. Sure enough, a newsbreak came. In Japanese.

"Pay attention, Kiko," I told the young girl. "I want to know what they're saying."

She listened. Her almond-shaped eyes widened. Her skin became chalky, the way Nashima's had become chalky when I'd asked her about the Sons.

"Mr. Holmes," she exploded. "The television says you are a dead man. Killed by a bomb in your hotel room. They're examining your body now."

EIGHT

The second day in the factory was no more fruit-ful than the first. Most of the employees glared at me suspiciously. Kiko had to serve as interpreter as I asked them a few questions about the explosion. Either they knew nothing or Kiko had screwed up the translation.

My meeting with Nato Nakuma was just as dis-couraging.

He was a gloomy-faced tyrant who ran a really taut ship in the toy factory. He didn't offer a hand-shake, and didn't give the traditional Japanese bow of greeting. He merely stood behind his great mahogany desk and glared at me with what can only be described as a dyspeptic look.

"You don't look like a toy salesman," he groused in faultless English.

"You don't look like a factory manager," I re-sponded, matching his gruffness. Neither of us said what the other really did look like, and it's just as well. The dialogue might have led to blows. "The point is," I added, "I am a toy salesman and I came to place an order for your robots. But only if

I can get a demonstration."

"You have not seen them work?"

"I haven't even been able to touch one of them."

He glared at Kiko and she looked ashamed of herself, even though I knew she'd been under his orders to keep me from touching the merchandise.

"Set up a demonstration," he commanded. "I will bring Mr. Holmes to the consultation room to see it in five minutes."

It was five minutes of discomfort. I asked Nato about the explosion, but he had no information.

"There are fifty other toy manufacturers in Japan," he said, still looking angry as though he'd like to strangle all fifty of them. "Of those, six are American companies. One of those six hired conspirators to learn the secret of Tikki-Tik. They sent—"

"Of who?"

"Tikki-Tik," he said. A smile almost but not quite crossed his lips. "It is the name of our splendid robot. Tikki-Tik. It makes that kind of sound as it moves. Clocklike, representing the precision that goes into its production."

"I see. You were saying about one of the American toymakers?"

"One of them sent conspirators to blow up our factory. They succeeded in blowing up the packing room of the American sector."

"The American sector?"

"To facilitate shipping," he said, sounding like a man who'd run out of patience, "we separate orders, depending on which country or region they will go to. All toys designated for the United States are channeled through one area. The same for other major buyers."

I was about to ask how many buyers they had for this amazing new robot, Tikki-Tik, but he moved around his desk—much like a robot—and steered me through a gaggle of glaring employees to the consultation room.

There, Kiko stood smiling alongside the little engineer, also smiling. On a long table was a robot, its little lights flashing. Its eyes were as green as jade, throwing beams of light across the room. I was reminded of that pleasant evening with Nashima, when I'd enjoyed adolescent stirrings of infatuation over the lovely woman who owned this factory.

Kiko stepped aside and Nato took over. He ran little Tikki-Tik through a series of maneuvers. It ticked like a clock. It did everything he asked of it, by voice command. Each time Nato shifted commands, Tikki-Tik responded with a polite bow, said in a clear robot's voice, "As you wish, sir," and then executed the new command.

The blasted thing did everything but jump off the table and fetch coffee.

"And now," Nato said, pride growing, "we shall show just why Tikki-Tik is far superior to other robots on the market. Tikki-Tik, I wish to discuss matters that would be comprehended by a five-year-old child with an IQ of, say, a hundred and ten."

"As you wish, sir," Tikki-Tik said, then proceeded to ramble on about family life, kindergarten, the alphabet, simple arithmetic, children's books, television.

"Enough," Nato cut the little codger off in midsentence. "You now must upgrade. You are now talking to a child of ten, with an IQ of a hundred and sixty."

Jesus, I thought. Genius class.

"As you wish, sir."

Tikki-Tik whizzed into a gabbling dissertation about Einstein's theory of relativity, nuclear physics, rocketry, space travel, opera, classical music and classical literature. Frankly, most of it sailed right over my head.

But one thing was clear. This was truly a superior toy, as Kiko had said. In fact, it was no toy. It was a highly sophisticated teaching tool that every kid in the world should have.

"Absolutely amazing," I said, reaching out to pick it up. "I'd expected something really great, but—"

I felt a hand on my arm, turned to see Nato Nakuma glaring at me. His hairy-fingered hand was restraining me.

"Please," he said, meaning something else entirely, "Tikki-Tik is not only sophisticated, he is delicate. I would ask that you not handle him."

"I was trying to determine how much the toy

weighs," I said. "My company is cost conscious, you know. And shipping costs are exorbitant."

"We have spec sheets giving all that data," Nato said. "I believe the spec sheets show that each Tikki-Tik weighs twenty pounds, without batteries. Each battery weighs one pound and there are four batteries in each robot."

"Thank you. You can let go of my arm now."

"Sorry."

He released his grip, but his eyes still warned me not to extend that arm any farther.

"You're pretty protective," I said, rubbing the arm where his tight grip had disturbed circulation. "Do you plan to go along with all these toys and keep the kids from playing with them? If they're so delicate, the average American child will have them destroyed five minutes after opening their Christmas packages."

"Full instructions on how to handle Tikki-Tik will accompany each toy," he said, emphasizing the word, "toy."

The demonstration was over. We left Tikki-Tik standing on the table, his lights flashing off and on, his bright green eyes staring after me. I got an eerie feeling from that. It was as though the robot were angry at me for standing up to his master, Nato Nakuma. Like a faithful dog.

I looked back. The green eyes were blazing into mine. I felt a kind of animosity in those twin beams of green light. I felt as though some alien force were beaming hatred, or death rays, at me.

The engineer who'd invented Tikki-Tik reached

out and flipped a switch on the robot's back. The lights went out, the eyes went black.

But I'd carry the memory of those haunting, threatening green lights for a long time.

I settled into the deep tub of hot water and let Kiko work magic on my neck and shoulders with her strong young hands. It had been a tiring and disappointing day. A traditional Japanese bath, in a deep tub with almost scalding water—and the attentive fingers of a naked young woman with skilled hands—was just what the doctor had ordered.

Nashima hadn't shown again at the office and I was beginning to wonder if something might be wrong with her. She had called and talked with Nato Nakuma and Kiko, but a call was a poor substitute for the real item, especially an item like Nashima who was pure joy to view.

And, of course, the news about what had happened at the hotel was upsetting. A maid had gone to my room to turn down the bed and had touched off the explosion rigged for me. They'd initially thought all those body parts belonged to me, but an autopsy proved it was the maid. I felt bad about that.

The biggest disappointment of the day was my failure to move my investigation off ground zero.

Except for my queer feelings about that amazing toy, feelings that stirred up disturbing thoughts about its powers, I'd learned nothing more about Tikki-Tik. Neither Kiko nor Nato knew the retail price of the toy, and Nato wasn't about to tell me how much it cost to produce it. I did learn the shipping date of the first batch going to the United States.

A whole warehouse full of the robots—two hundred thousand of them—was to be loaded aboard a ship on November 1st—just a week away. The ship would reach San Francisco by November 15th and the first batch of toys would be in stores across the country by the end of the month.

That made it a bit late for the usual Christmas rush, but an advertising campaign that was to begin the day the toys left Japan would whet the appetites of American kids so that, by the time the toys were available, virtually all of them would be immediately bought by adoring, pampering parents.

Three days after the first shipment—and each three days after that—another two hundred thousand robots would be shipped. By the final shopping week before Christmas, there would be upward of two million Tikki-Tiks all packaged and ready to put under American Christmas trees.

Tumio was birddogging the advertising agency in Tokyo to make certain the word got out at the proper time. Literally millions, Kiko said, were being spent on the ad campaign.

And yet, nobody seemed to know what the toy would cost.

And I didn't believe this.

I also didn't believe what Nato had told me about the weight of each robot. Twenty pounds seemed damned heavy to me. Make that twenty-four pounds with batteries.

Thirty years ago, such a toy would have weighed a hundred pounds, but they didn't have computer chips, sophisticated computer circuitry and super-strong, lightweight space metals in the fifties. At top, I figured, Tikki-Tik should weigh no more than eight to ten pounds. Possibly even less.

But that was hardly anything to worry about. The big item was cost. I knew little about toys, but a few things about computerized equipment. Even a small hand calculator used to tote up numbers cost upward of thirty or forty dollars. An old-fashioned rocking horse, with no batteries and no brains, computer or otherwise, cost from fifty bucks upward.

Tikki-Tik, I reasoned, had to sell for two or three hundred dollars. Perhaps even more. Sophisticated toy or not, how the hell were they hoping to sell nearly two million of those toys in America—in so short a time?

Other questions buzzed through my mind. Why had Nato had workmen strip away the evidence of the explosion so fast? There hadn't even been an investigation by the Hiroshima bomb squad. The explosion hadn't been reported to the police. Why not? I didn't buy Nashima's claim that acts of violence between competing companies were kept strictly in the family.

"You look very worried," Kiko said as she moved the harsh bar of soap and cloth from my shoulders down across my chest. "Am I doing a lousy job?"

"It's a great bath," I said.

"Good. Now for some fun."

Before I could object that I was still drained from last night, she leaped into the tub with me. She pressed her supple body into me, rubbed those fine young breasts against my chest and slid her thigh far up between my legs.

In spite of my fatigue, and the questions and doubts buzzing through my mind, I felt myself being aroused. I just hoped that I'd have enough energy for what I had to do tonight.

There were too many questions and too few answers. As soon as Kiko was asleep, I planned to go out to the factory on my own. The worst that could happen, I reasoned, was that I'd come back empty-handed, with no answers to my questions.

NINE

After an assault at the airport and two explosions in hotel rooms I'd reserved, I figured my cover was blown enough to go out and rent a car. I now headed the little Toyota down toward the industrial section, crossing bridge after bridge, being grateful that it was past midnight and most of Hiroshima's drivers were home in bed.

The factory was dark, closed down for the night in spite of the urgency to get more Tikki-Tiks made for shipment to America and other countries. I shut off the headlights a block from the factory, slowed the Toyota to a crawl and stopped a hundred feet shy of the main gate.

I knew there would be a guard at the gate, but doubted that the whole premises would be patrolled. I was right. At the rear, just beyond the warehouse, I found a place where the barbed wire on top of the chainlink fence was slack. I climbed up, parted the wire and slipped through.

There were lights here and there in the huge factory compound. Most of them were on poles, but the warehouse had lights at each corner of the vast roof. I found shadows, crept through them and neared the wing where robots were being prepared for shipment to America. I don't know why, but I felt that that wing would provide the answers I sought—if, indeed, there *were* any answers.

As I approached the wing, a light suddenly went on in a small office inside. I could see from the distance that the working area of the packing and shipping section had dim lights, but the bright light coming on so suddenly startled me.

I backed off and waited. From my vantage point near the warehouse, hiding in the shadow of huge crates, I could see movement in that office. People were moving about, talking, gesturing. A blind had been pulled just after the light went on, so I could see only silhouettes of waving arms, bobbing heads, moving torsos.

After waiting a few minutes, I decided I'd better get a closer look. I reached the window, but it was too high for me to catch details of sounds oozing through the shaded glass. I found a box, placed it beneath the window and stood on it. I pressed my ear to the glass; the words were English.

". . . no reason to suspect that he is anything but a toy salesman," Nato Nakuma was saying. "We spend no more time on him. Production is the main thing. I have arranged for the ships to leave every two days after November 1st. With increased production, we can have . . ."

I didn't get to hear any more.

There was movement behind me and to my

right. I turned and, sure enough, men were approaching.

A quick count ticked off seven of them. They were all wearing black hoods, but none of them seemed to have weapons.

They were closing in on me, in a semicircle, each man walking in a crouch with hands outstretched, like a gorilla.

I was reaching for Wilhelmina when the nearest man made his move. He swept in so close that I could see his eyes sparkling through the holes in the black hood.

"Hai, hai!" he cried as he lunged at me.

He came feet first. Wilhelmina was out of its holster, but not yet in firing position, when two bare but very hard feet crashed into my throat.

Even as I tumbled off the box, I felt the pain searing my throat, all the way from the back of my tongue to my lungs. And I could hardly breathe. I brought the Luger into the open and was aiming up at the black-hooded man's right eye when a second man moved in with flying feet. He kicked the Luger from my hand with one foot and cracked me in the side of the head with the other. How he worked those feet so fast, I'll never know, but the blows came almost simultaneously.

Fighting unconsciousness and still trying to get a breath through my agonized trachea, I rolled over on the ground and struggled to my feet just as two other men came at me, feet first.

I had Hugo in hand by then. I used him.

Four well-trained feet that had hoped to snap my spine and crush my skull immediately went out of action. I worked the stiletto quickly, turning and stabbing. Blood spurted from all four feet and the men screamed in pain and anger. At least they could scream. I couldn't even breathe.

I sensed movement behind me and turned as three men came rushing in, their hands up in the classic judo stance. I waved Hugo at them. They glanced down at their fallen comrades, saw the blood soaking the dark earth and had second thoughts.

Instead of attacking, they circled me, forcing me more and more into the open area beyond the wing of the building. I kept whirling around as each man feinted with his hands and moved in and out.

The breath of life finally began to come easier through my damaged trachea. Adrenaline pumped viciously in my blood and I felt that I could take all these men at once. Especially with two of them out of action.

But there were five men circling me now, edging me farther and farther into the open. One got too bold in his feints, moved too close, and I damned near took off his thumb. His scream must have been heard all the way to the center of the city. Yet, inside, the figures kept posturing behind the shade, the discussion about production and shipping still going on. Surely, they must have heard the screams, grunts and slamming about.

But then, why would they bother to come outside to the defense of a man who'd just broken into their factory? Especially after someone had blown up a section of the packing and shipping room in one of the five factory wings.

There were only four men in the circle now. The two with slashed feet were leaning against the building, nursing their wounds. The man with the severed thumb was bending over, holding it tightly to stem the flow of blood.

I looked around at the four black-hooded men, assessing their strengths and weaknesses, looking for the slowest.

I found him, a fat little man who kept stumbling over his own feet, and I lunged toward him, swishing Hugo violently. With a nimbleness that surprised me, he leaped back. Hugo slashed empty air.

In that moment of vulnerability, the other three closed in. Blows came like shrapnel from a newly exploded grenade. I caught three hand slashes to the throat, closing off my breathing again. A fourth blow caught me in the back of the neck and I heard my spine rattle all the way down to my tailbone.

Then came the stomach blow, from a flying, plunging foot.

All the lights in the universe seemed to flash through my head then. I bent over to vomit, only to feel three rapid blows to the back of my neck. One of the men hit me in the back of the legs, taking my props from beneath me. Another grabbed my right wrist and, with a vicious, twisting motion, nearly snapped off my hand.

Hugo went tumbling to the ground.

Blows kept coming. I kept going down and

getting up. Finally, I went down and had no more energy to rise.

That didn't stop the blows. They were getting more serious now, going for vital organs. I felt three to my right kidney before the lights of the universe began to flicker out, by tens and twenties.

There was a respite from the blows. I could hear the men panting from their violent efforts. I felt consciousness coming and going, heard pleasant voices, then harsh panting.

And then, as though renewed by a change of seasons, the men came at me with their well-trained hands and feet again.

On the seventh punch to the right kidney, I felt consciousness leaving for good.

I opened my eyes, saw someone move past the shade in the lighted office, saw hands go up in some kind of angry gesture, then closed my eyes and dropped off the edge of the earth.

Later, but not much later, I felt movement, heard the high-pitched whine of a small engine. I was in a car. In the trunk. I could feel the spare tire against my spine. My head lay in a pool of something warm. My own blood.

I passed out again.

The next time I awoke, light was streaming through a window. It looked like a window, and yet it wasn't a window. On closer examination by my swollen, aching eyes, I saw that it was a hole in the wall. A jagged hole.

I groaned and moved my head. The movement sent pain up and down my body, reminding my brain that pain had been there all along.

All around me on a wooden floor were chunks of debris, most of it charred, as though a furious fire or intense heat had at one time been in or close to this building.

I gazed at the ceiling. Wooden timbers showed through broken plaster. I could see into a room above, and a room above that. Beyond at least three floors was a roof. There were jagged holes in that roof, letting in light from the sky.

My first thought was that I was in a hotel, that I had miraculously survived a tremendous explosion. It was like being left behind in a part of hell that had been abandoned by others as an intolerable place to exist.

There was no furniture in the room. It had been consumed in the fire or blown through the walls and ceiling by the explosion.

Suddenly, I knew where I was.

The old ruins at one end of Peace Park.

The building that had been gutted by the atomic bomb blast of more than thirty-five years ago and left as a memorial to that holocaust.

The building that was off-limits to visitors. No one ever came inside this building. In time, it would tumble into a pile of rubble all on its own.

And I knew then that the black-hooded men had left me alive so that I could suffer and die in this empty, abandoned, unvisited building.

Repayment, retribution, a symbolic eye-for-an-eye gesture.

One more victim of the A-bomb blast that took

seventy-five thousand lives in the twinkling of an eye, and left tens of thousands more to die of burns and radiation.

And that victim was to be me, Nick Carter, N3, Killmaster for AXE.

Not, by God, if I could help it.

I moved my head again, trying to see through the gaping hole to my right.

Pain rattled up and down my body. My kidneys came alive with complaint. Agonizing complaint.

Again and again, I tried to move various parts of my body. Movement of my head set off all sorts of pains. The same thing happened when I tried to move my hands and legs. Jesus, I couldn't even swivel my eyeballs without setting off rockets of agony damned near everywhere in my body.

I stopped trying to move. Give it time, my mind said. In time, maybe only an hour or so, I'll get the hell out of here and find help.

The hunger pangs found their way through all that pain. Thirst was rampant. Christ, had I lost so much blood that I was literally dying of hunger and dehydration?

No. I'd lost only a little blood, through my nose. There were no open wounds that a mental check of my body could detect.

The deep hunger and parching thirst came from one thing.

Time.

I had apparently been in this building for some time. Perhaps days. The light of the sky was not merely the dawn of the day after my visit to the factory and my encounter with those seven men.

It was the middle of the second, third, fourth or fifth day.

No. The human body can go without water no more than seventy-two hours. Some anxious sense deep inside me told me that I had used up most, if not all, of that time by being totally unconscious.

I tried to scream, to attract attention. Peace Park was always full of visitors. Someone would hear, call the police. It was better to rest in a Japanese jail as a fugitive from immigration—having entered the country with a false passport—than to die of thirst in this ruin from the first A-bomb blast.

Nothing but pain came from my throat. My lips, swollen and bloody from the beating and from thirst, barely parted for sound that would not come.

I tried the moving bit again with the same agonizing results. I passed out several times from sheer pain.

Panic threatened to take control.

Once or twice, I slept and dreamed how pleasant it would be to simply die and escape all this pain. A sense of euphoria overcame me and I knew that I was in danger.

Wishing to die is the final step before death itself.

But the euphoria was strong, overcoming my sense of danger.

I lay still, no longer fighting, no longer trying to move, welcoming death, wishing it would hurry.

TEN

Darkness came. Several hours had passed while I was asleep. I recalled having awakened, disappointed that death hadn't come, then falling asleep again. Now, I was fully awake and there was moonlight streaming in through the roof, through the gaping hole to my right.

I turned my head and looked at the hole in the side of the building. The pain that rumbled up and down my body was endurable. Just barely. I gazed at the silent bell tower at the opposite end of the park.

Civilization was out there, just a few hundred feet away. The park was empty, but surely there would be someone near to hear my shouts.

I tried again to call out, but nothing came. Not even a hoarse whisper.

I moved my feet, one at a time. Then a hand, and the other. The pain was there, but not nearly as bad as it had been earlier. I lifted my head again and held it there until I felt myself going unconscious. I put my head down, the pain eased and consciousness returned fully.

For the next several hours, I kept moving various parts of my body. Gradually, the pain eased off and I was able to rise to a sitting position without passing out.

My spine felt as though it had been taken apart and put back together by a burly child with careless fingers. Both kidneys ached like rotted teeth, and I had wet myself a number of times. If the building hadn't been so wide open with holes from the bomb blast and the elements, the place would have stunk to high heaven.

First light was beginning to show in the east when I finally got up the nerve to try to move. I pulled myself with my hands, pushing only a little with my knees.

The pain was excruciating and I passed out for short intervals. Finally, though, I was moving along as fast as a reasonably healthy snail.

I reached a doorway and was looking into a wide corridor filled with debris. Beyond, seemingly miles away, was a stair railing. I edged toward it and, sure enough, there were stairs.

I was on the third floor, afraid to start down those steps. If I slipped and fell, I'd finish the job those black-hooded men had started.

It was a chance I had to take.

I sat at the top of the stairs, kicked aside debris and moved down on my butt, one step at a time. I clung to railings when there were railings. I made it to the front door just as the sun was turning eastern clouds to pink and orange and fuchsia.

It had never looked more beautiful, that rising sun.

I waited a few minutes and tried my feet. I stood for a moment, felt myself passing out and dropped to my butt on the front steps of the ruins. A policeman walked by, a hundred yards distant. I tried to call out to him. A hoarse whisper emerged from my swollen lips. No more.

The sun had already topped the nearest buildings, a huge red ball like a toy balloon, by the time I could take a few steps. I stumbled along, fell repeatedly, got up and went on.

Across a wide lawn . . . past a fountain . . . past benches. I rested for a moment, then went on, finally reaching the street. A few cars lurched along blindly, horns blowing. At the corner, a traffic light turned red. I waited for a break in traffic and started across the street.

The light turned and cars came at me, horns blowing. I tried to run, but could only move in slow motion. The cars came faster, bearing down on me.

With immense effort, I forced my feet to move faster. I lunged forward and just managed to fall onto the sidewalk as a whole line of horn-blowing Toyotas and Datsuns swept past my feet, swirling dust.

I heard a voice nearby, speaking softly in Japanese.

I rolled to my back and looked up into the face of a kindly old man with a cane. He had a wispy gray beard and a black hat.

I shook my head, indicating that I didn't understand him. I made the universal gesture of a man talking on a telephone. I whispered.

"I want to get to a telephone."

"Ah, telephone. Come. Into my shop."

I had hit it lucky. Not only did the old man speak English, but he had a jewelry shop right in front of where I'd fallen to escape the rumbling traffic.

He unlocked the door, led me inside, took off his black hat and showed me the telephone. I sat at his desk, gazed foggily at his jeweler's tools and picked up the receiver. I'd memorized Nashima's home number, but my memory failed me now.

"Nashima Porfiro," I whispered to the old man.

"Ah. Nashima Porfiro. Toy family."

"Yes," I said. "Toy family."

He looked up the number, dialed it and handed me the receiver. Nashima's soft voice answered. I whispered as loud as I could.

"This is Peter Holmes. I'm in trouble. Can you come get me?"

Nashima apparently hadn't heard a word I'd said. She rattled in Japanese. I was getting anxious, angry. I tried to whisper louder. Finally, the old man took the receiver.

"This is Peter Holmes," he said in perfect imitation of my plea. "I'm in trouble. Can you come get me?"

I could hear Nashima speaking English now,

puzzled by the strange voice using my name. The old man responded in Japanese and, soon, they had a lively conversation going. The old man hung up.

"Little confusion," he said, smiling at me. "You come lay on cot in back. Lady come soon. I fix good."

In twenty minutes, while the old jeweler was trying to get some water down my throat, and failing miserably, Nashima breezed into the shop with a huge man she said was her servant.

The servant, a big, empty-eyed man with a bald head and a sweet, endearing smile, scooped me from the cot and carried me outside to a huge Lincoln Continental. I looked back and saw Nashima trying to give the old jeweler money, but he refused it.

Less than a half hour later, I was in a hospital bed, rigged up to IV bottles that were providing nourishment and painkillers. X-rays had revealed that no bones were broken, but there was damage to both kidneys and my spleen. There was internal bleeding.

Nashima sat beside my bed, shushing me when I tried to talk, and in a few minutes I felt the euphoria again. I slept like the dead.

In the middle of the afternoon, I was almost back to par. Nashima had left and come back. The big man-servant remained in the room with us, smiling his endearing smile.

"I've searched for you for three days," Nashima said. "The doctors now say that you're able to tell me what happened. Without damaging your throat, that is."

I told her about my night visit to the factory, the meeting going on behind that closed shade, the assault of the seven black-hooded men, my awakening in the ruined building of Peace Park and my struggle to get to a telephone. She sat for a long time when I had finished whispering out the story. That dark cloud passed behind her eyes a number of times as I mentioned different points. I tried to remember just which points made her react that way, but my mind was in too much of a muddle.

The telling of the story exhausted me. I fell back to sleep, awakening again when it was dark outside. Nashima was there, sitting in the chair beside the bed, another lovely silk kimono flowing along the exquisite lines of her body. The manservant, named Toko, hovered in the background.

"I have arranged for you to be flown to America the first thing in the morning," Nashima said. "I spoke with David Hawk this afternoon. He agrees. It is our mutual assessment that the attacks on you by the Sons of August Six may not have anything to do with the explosion at Porfiro Toy Factory. Even if they are, your cover has been blown, as Hawk said, so that you are no longer an effective investigator."

I was in no mood to argue. Even with painkillers, the pain was running amok in my body. Even with the IVs, I felt hungry and thirsty. But something in me made me argue.

"No dice on the plane home," I said, surprised that my voice rose above a whisper. "Those attacks have a direct bearing on the toy factory explosion. You know it. I know it. Hawk knows it. I don't know why he agreed to pull me out."

She bowed her head, then smiled into my eyes. I saw that the piece of jade was still in her hair. "Perhaps to save your life," she said in a soft voice. "Listen. Don't interrupt now. I have spoken with Nato Nakuma at the factory about the assault on you by those men. He knows nothing of the fight. He heard nothing. As for the meeting, it was quite legitimate. We are behind schedule. The meeting was to determine whether to start up extra shifts at the factory."

"They were talking about me," I said. "What do I have to do with production and extra shifts?"

"Perhaps you misunderstood what you heard." She looked away, unable to meet my eyes. "It is settled. You leave at nine o'clock tomorrow morning. The doctors have said you will be able to travel by then, as long as we take you in a wheelchair and—"

"And what happens here?" I interrupted. "Suppose the people who set off that first explosion come back to blow up the whole damned factory and all the people in it? Suppose—"

"That is not to be your concern," Nashima said firmly. "You were sent here as a favor to me. I withdraw the request. I will tell what I know to the police and let them handle it."

"And what will you say to the Sons of August

Six who have threatened you if you go to the authorities?''

Her face dropped, her eyes showed panic, even terror.

"It is not to be your concern."

I thought of all that had happened since I'd left San Francisco five days ago. "I think it's my concern," I said. "Okay, you asked Hawk for a favor and he complied. I'm that favor. But I haven't finished my own work, much less yours. I'll stay, Nashima, not so much to help you as to get to the bottom of something that's touched me very personally and painfully."

"No," she said. "You leave in the morning, even if I have to bring all my man-servants down here and have them carry you aboard that plane. It is settled."

She stood up, as if to go. I waved her back down. "All right. You win. I'll be ready to go in the morning. Meanwhile, sit down and answer some questions for me. There are some things I need to find out before I go home with my tail between my legs."

She sat down. Her smile was apprehensive, as if I were trying to pull a fast one on her. In point of fact, I was.

When Nashima heard the questions, a dark cloud seemed to pass behind her lovely eyes. Suddenly, she got up, tears in her eyes.

"I don't know the answers," she blurted. "It doesn't matter. You're on the wrong track. Besides, you're going home first thing in the morning, so it's all academic."

With that, she ran out of the room.

And I knew that I would not be going home in the morning. Not if she brought along all the manservants in Japan to haul my ass aboard that plane.

Because, for one thing, I knew I was on the right track. And that track, if it led where I thought it would lead, would take me to one of the most grisly plots in the history of mankind.

And, most probably, to my death.

ELEVEN

It wasn't until three in the morning that the nurse and doctor came to remove the IV needles, putting me on my own as far as nourishment and liquids were concerned. Thankfully, the nurse gave me a pain shot just before the two left me to sleep through the night.

I battled sleep. I had other plans.

At a quarter of four, with darkness running out fast, I sat up on the bed and let the room spin itself out. It took me ten minutes to get myself to my feet, another ten to find my clothes in a white metal cabinet. My wallet and money were there, but no weapons.

At precisely four-thirty, I moved past the final nurses' station where there was virtually no activity, and made it to the front door. Taxis were whirling along the streets, and I hailed one easily.

"Hakasu-dori Bridge," I said as plainly as I possibly could.

The driver didn't understand. Hakasu-dori is a very long street that connects three of the six islands of the city. There were probably two dozen bridges along its path. Luckily, I'd been driving Kiko's battered Buick around the city, not riding as a passenger. I knew the way.

With gestures and generous hunks of yen, I managed to make the taxi driver understand. By five o'clock, we were where I wanted to be: in the heart of a seedy, derelict-ridden section of cheap shops and hotels. Near the bridge connecting the southernmost islands. All the eighty bridges in the city have names, but I'd forgotten this one.

General Sikora Bridge, the sign said. I wouldn't forget it again.

Shortly after five-thirty, I settled in a tiny room on the fourth floor of a hotel building that was only a half-notch better than the ruined building of Peace Park. But the bed was soft enough, and I pulled the shade on the single window to assure privacy and continued darkness.

I slept then, awakening at noon. I was weak from hunger and thirst. I had to walk the four flights down to the main desk where, with gestures and yen, I managed to send out for food and drink.

Back in the room I ate, drank, slept again. The next morning, twenty-four hours after I was supposed to have been on a plane back to the States, I awoke alert. Slept out. No more drugs in my system. The pain was just short of exquisite.

Pain or not, time was running out. In just four days, that ship would leave for the States. I had to move fast.

I took another taxi to the area of the Porfiro Toy Factory and, sure enough, there was my rented Toyota on the side street where I'd parked it the night those black-hooded thugs beat me senseless.

The factory compound was bustling with activity as workers hauled huge wooden crates from the factory to the warehouse. The crates, I presumed, were filled with boxed and packaged Tikki-Tiks. I had a sudden thought, so I set off in the little rented car.

On the northernmost island was a small airport used exclusively for private and chartered aircraft. I'd seen it on the city map provided along with Hawk's initial instructions. It occurred to me that I might be able to rent a small plane or helicopter, both of which I could fly—though not as an expert.

As soon as I drove onto the airport grounds, I spotted the sign: KAI TAI'S FLYING SERVICE.

Beneath the sign was a smaller one, listing the various aircraft available for rent or for lessons. Bell helicopters were among them, a type I was familiar with. Especially Cobras.

Kai Tai was a small, grease-covered man who scowled all the time and spoke a wild pidgin English.

"Showing license please, costing maybe ten thousand yen," he rattled, wiping grease from a big wrench. "No license, costing twenty thousand down payment cash right now, one hour usage."

I paid him the twenty thousand, about a hundred dollars, for a small, two-seater Bell Aircoupe.

"You wreck," he said, threatening with the wrench, "come day judgmentlike over head of Yankee slime. Understandable, we got deal."

I peeled off twenty thousand yen and helped him push the little Aircoupe out onto the tarmac. In ten minutes, I was out over the Ota River, nearing the factory grounds.

I stayed at five thousand feet, high enough to eliminate suspicion from below, low enough to see individual figures in the factory compound.

It didn't take long to spot the guards mingling in with the workers. I counted twelve of them, all with rifles. As I was circling for another look, a huge semi-truck left the warehouse, cruised down an alley and started up the main street. I hovered high above, watching it as it turned toward the main docks on the Ota River.

There, the truck nestled up near a long, dark freighter. I dipped the little chopper to the east and came in low, to read the markings on the freighter. It was the *Endiro Gotsu.*

From the looks of all the activity below, the ship seemed almost ready to embark on its voyage to San Francisco. Even as I watched stevedores begin to unload the first truck, another truck arrived.

My hour was about up, but I still wanted to check out those guards at the factory. I zoomed back south, came in at a low angle to get a really good look, and that's when I learned all I needed to know about the rifles the guards were carrying.

Six of them cut loose at the same time. I saw the tongues of flame and, before I could twist the throttle to full and ram forward the cyclic pitch stick to get the hell out of there, I felt the thud of a bullet somewhere back near the copter's tail.

Kai Tai was nowhere around when I returned his damaged chopper. I set it down near his hangar, walked painfully to my car and drove away.

Back at the crummy hotel, I called Nashima.

"Nick, where in the devil are you? Why did you leave the hospital? Don't you know that, without medication, poison from your damaged kidneys can spread through your body and—"

"Nashima," I said, cutting her off. "I want to get into the factory, especially the packing room and the warehouse. I want to run a comparison study."

"A what?"

"You know what a comparison study is," I said. "And I don't have to tell you what I want to compare."

"Nick, you're crazy. There's nothing to your wild theory. Take my word for it, there's—"

"I'm not taking anybody's word for anything," I said. "Are you aware that Nato Nakuma has the whole factory under heavy guard? Or did you put them there yourself?"

"I can't get you inside the factory because I have no power in the matter."

"I don't understand."

"When my husband died, the board of directors made Nato Nakuma the real head of the company.

Because of the Porfiro name, I was given the title of president. But I am an executive in name only. I have no power. That's why I don't keep regular office hours. I was going insane down in that office with nothing to do. As for the warehouse, Mr. Nick Carter, only a few hand-picked men are allowed there. I am not among the chosen."

"And the hand picking is done by Nato, right?"

"Yes."

"So, all you could do when the explosion came was call David Hawk in hopes your old friend from America could solve your problems."

"Please, there's no need to be sarcastic. I simply have no power in the matter."

I was trying not to lose respect for this woman. I couldn't believe that a woman of her strength and composure would sit still for a figurehead job so long, let her name but not her talents be used. I told her as much.

"You have to understand the role of the woman in Japan," she said. "Although we've advanced considerably since World War Two, there is still a vast difference between Japan and the United States as it concerns women's rights. To be head of such a large factory is an honorable position for a woman in—"

"No job without substance has any honor," I snapped. "See you around, lady."

My next call was to Tumio, in Tokyo. Since he was only a vice president, and obviously banished to the Tokyo office, he probably had less power than Nashima. I didn't expect much help. But I needed only one small bit of information.

He went through the same bunch of questions Nashima had. I cut him short, asked him directly: "What's the robot going to sell for in America?"

"You left the hospital and went into hiding just to ask me that?"

"No. I have a number of other things to do, have other questions to ask. That one just happens to be pertinent to a theory I have in mind. Do you know the cost?"

"I think it would be a good idea for you to return to the hospital," he said. "Or go see Nashima and let her arrange your flight home. I can meet you here again and facilitate the change of flights, if you wish."

"I don't wish," I snapped. "Look, Tumio, I'm in so damned much pain that I really don't know why I care anymore about your fucking factory. Or you or Nashima or anybody or anything. You're probably all involved in this thing, all members of the Sons of August Six, for all I know. Maybe I'm talking to the wrong people. Maybe I should go to the police and take my chances on having one of the Sons find out. I don't know. I do know that something really rotten is in the works and I need some data. One piece of data concerns how much that robot is going to sell for in America. Do you know?"

There was a pause. I think I really nicked him with the implication that he and Nashima were members of the Sons of August Six.

"I don't know it," he said, "but the advertising

department has prepared secret materials to be flown to the United States tomorrow. I can try to get a peek at that material."

So, he also had a job without substance. Well, so what?

"I'll call you back this evening," I said. "Give me a time when you'll be in your apartment."

"I'll call you," he said, in a cautious, frightened voice.

"No dice. Give me a time."

He argued until I was convinced that both he and Nashima were under a death threat from the Sons. But he gave me a time—nine o'clock.

I left the phone booth, found a decent-looking restaurant and ate until I thought I would burst. I was weak from hunger, and a fever was nibbling at my heels. Or maybe it was poison from my kidneys, as Nashima had said.

It didn't matter. They'd hold out for four days. Maybe even less time was needed. I'd heard Nato Nakuma say he'd try to speed up the frequency of shipments after the first one—maybe he'd also speed up the first one, make it on October 29th or 30th. I had to find out.

From the restaurant, I called the Japanese Coast Guard and learned that the *Endiro Gotsu* was still scheduled to sail on November 1st.

Okay, I had the four days. But would my kidneys hold out? From the pain down there and the growing fever, I doubted it. I drank two bottles of sake, hating every swallow of it, to hold off the thirst and put a damper on the pain.

The sake did neither, but I felt better for having downed it and gotten it out of the way.

I made another slow survey of the factory grounds, saw the guards with their rifles, knew they were young and inexperienced, then went back to the hotel to get some rest. I awoke shortly before nine, went down to the lobby and called Tumio.

There was no hello, no greeting of any kind. I heard a click when someone picked up the phone, then heard Tumio's voice, high and strained, blurt: "Eight thousand yen."

And then the phone went dead. Jesus, the guy was really running scared.

I made a quick calculation. Eight thousand yen checked out at around forty dollars, depending on the rate of exchange on any given day.

So, that was the price of the toy in America. A damned good price.

I was just starting to hang up the dead phone and return to my room and map strategy when I caught movement from the corner of my eye. I kept the phone at my ear, turned slowly.

Three men in black hoods were at the desk, questioning a chalk-skinned, frightened clerk. I turned my face to the wall and waited. I heard their heavy footsteps, turned to see them going up the stairs.

I let them go. This was no time for a pitched battle with three goons trained in judo, kung fu and jujitsu. I slipped from the booth and, while the clerk stood gazing frightenedly up the staircase after the intruders, I slipped out and got into my rented Toyota.

But where to?

Maybe I'd be welcome at Nashima's house, maybe not. If she were under a death threat, her house would be watched. It obviously was, as was her phone, or they wouldn't have been able to track me to that sleezy hotel. Then again, they could have tracked me through Tumio, or Tumio himself could have traced the call and sent the Sons of August Six after me.

There was only one place where I could feel reasonably safe. My body might not be able to stand the stress, but maybe I'd find a way around the inevitable.

I'd go to Kiko Shoshoni.

TWELVE

"Where have you been for the past two days?" Kiko demanded, her face beaming with delight as I stood in her open doorway. "I've been calling everywhere, hoping to find you—with no luck. Anyway, I'm happy to see you."

It took a few minutes to get her quieted down. Still, she chattered on and on as she prepared a bath, which I sorely needed. Even she could tell by looking at me that I was in no condition for love-making.

After expecting me at the factory again, she had called everyone she knew to find out where I'd gone. She'd even called Nashima who, for reasons of her own, hadn't told Kiko that I'd been beaten and had left the hospital against the advice of doctors.

I told Kiko of the beating, watching her face for reaction. There was only concern, pity, surprise and outrage. Unless, of course, she was a superb actress.

I finally got through to her the fact that I

needed sanctuary, then weapons. She agreed to help, to tell no one that I was in her apartment.

"And that includes Nashima," I said.

Her eyes widened in surprise. "Not tell honorable boss-lady?"

"Must not tell *anyone*," I said, hissing my words for emphasis.

She gazed at me, empty-eyed, then nodded. "Okay."

The bath went well. I felt far better. Kiko had a bottle of aspirin and I took a handful. She had no sleeping pills, but her gentle massaging soon had me sound asleep.

I awoke to full light. Kiko was gone, obviously to the factory. I had entertained the idea of having the girl get me into the factory at night, but I was doubtful of her naiveté. And there was no sense getting the innocent girl in trouble with the Sons.

As the hours passed in her quiet, comfortable apartment and I began to feel stronger, a sense of danger came over me. I've known for years that people do things differently in the Orient, that the enigmatic is somewhat common. But the enigma of what was happening here—who was doing what to whom and when and why—was more than my mind could take. Paranoia set in, coming in gallops. By noon, I felt unsafe in Kiko's apartment, imagining that she was telling everyone she knew about the American toy salesman she had stashed away.

I scribbled a note, telling her that I'd check

with her later, then went out to the Toyota.

A half-hour later, I was back in the old section near the hotel where I'd been staying. I avoided the hotel, heading for a particular shop down under the bridge. It was the closest thing to an American pawn shop that the Japanese have.

For fifty thousand yen, I bought a .45 caliber automatic that looked as though it might work with a little coddling. The shop owner was so pleased that I didn't haggle on the price that he threw in five extra clips, plus a neat eight-inch hunting knife in a leather sheath. The Sheffield steel blade had been made in England.

I cruised around the city most of the afternoon and, about dinnertime, settled on a small hotel on the northernmost island. It wasn't the seedy ruins I'd slept in earlier, and it wasn't the classy digs I'd tried to stay in before. It was small and inexpensive and quiet, one of a dozen just like it.

I checked in under another name, went to the room and called Kiko. The chatter began. I shut it off.

"Sorry to bug out on you like that," I said, "but I had my reasons. I'm feeling much better and I have some questions I'd like to ask you. Can you come to my hotel?"

"Sure. Just tell me where."

I gave her directions to a hotel on a middle island, told her where to park her battered Buick, told her to stay in the car. I had no reason to suspect that the girl was part of the strange conspiracy, but she could have talked, could be followed.

I drove to the appointed location and, sure enough, she was there. I checked out the area. No suspicious persons around. In fact, there were virtually no cars at all on the spacious parking lot. The few cars that were there were empty. I checked them all.

And then I picked up Kiko and took her to my new hotel room.

We made love. More correctly, she made love. I wasn't much of a contributor to the deed, but she didn't seem to mind. This kid was one of the greatest self-motivated dynamos I'd ever encountered.

I hit her with a few questions about the factory, about Nato Nakuma, about the Sons of August Six. Again, either she was thoroughly ignorant of any wrongdoing, or she was a classy actress.

Even so, as I began to drift off to sleep with Kiko in my arms, I felt uneasy. My mind tried to trace the source of the uneasiness, then concluded that a man in my position had reason to feel uneasy.

The past few days had been no joyride. The next few promised to be even worse. I'd have been totally insane not to feel uneasy.

I awoke, restless, sometime during the night and had the feeling that I was alone in the bed. Maybe Kiko had gotten up and returned to her apartment. I was too drowsy to think beyond that, so I went back to sleep.

Some time later, I came slightly awake, heard a board squeak somewhere in the room. Street lamps spilled inadequate light into the room, but I could see that someone was approaching the bed. That someone had arms raised. There was something in the hands, something that glinted.

I'd slipped the old .45 under my pillow, but my hand had eased on it during sleep. My fingers gripped it tightly now and I spun out of bed so fast that I thought both my kidneys had burst from the effort.

"Hai!"

The battle cry of the samurai shrieked in the room. It was followed quickly by a sickening thunk of something plunging into the pillow I'd just evacuated.

I rolled away from the bed and came up with the .45 in my hands. The figure across the bed raised the sword again and I was ready to pull the trigger when something about the shape and size of the person in the room made me wait.

"Kiko? Kiko, is that you?"

It was.

The girl dropped the sword to the floor and collapsed crying on the bed. I got up slowly, nursing the new pains that wracked my body. I approached cautiously, went around the bed to the window, closed the shade, turned on a lamp and looked down at the sword.

It was beautiful, richly decorated, a true samurai's weapon.

Kiko was sobbing wildly now, thrashing about on the bed, babbling about her poor sisters and brothers, her poor parents, her poor grandparents, her poor uncles and aunts and cousins.

I didn't need to be hit with a hammer to guess what she was babbling about. But I had to hear it from her.

I stuck the .45 into a drawer and went to sit on the bed beside the hysterical girl. I pulled her to a sitting position, held her gently to me, stroked her hair and spoke soothingly. When her sobbing diminished, I said in a whisper.

"All right, Kiko, let's talk. This time, I want answers to all my questions."

THIRTEEN

The girl took a lot of calming. Even then, she seemed reluctant to talk.

"All right," I said, "maybe I can speed things along. You're under a death threat from the Sons of August Six, aren't you?"

She sat bolt upright. Her eyes, always so full of love and impishness, were fiery with fright.

"How did you know?"

I sighed. "I have a feeling that half the people in Japan have been threatened by the Sons. Tell me how they managed to get you to try this stupid trick."

It wasn't really a stupid trick. If I hadn't been uneasy last night before falling asleep, hadn't awakened to find her gone, I might have been sleeping soundly. The "trick" would have worked. I'd be playing the role of the headless horseman— without a horse.

Kiko told me what had been happening with her.

Three hooded men had come to her apartment the evening after I'd left to check out the factory.

They'd told her that I was an enemy of the emperor and must be eradicated. She had to help, or she and her whole family—the entire bloodline—would be wiped out in the name of the emperor.

For the next two days, she kept looking for me, unaware that I was in the hospital, badly beaten by other black-hooded gentlemen. When I came to her apartment, she disobeyed orders and didn't tell the hooded visitors that I was there. In fact, she told no one.

But the men suspected. They called on her during her lunch hour, accosting her just outside the factory. She was to do me in that night. When she came home and found me gone, she was frantic. The men had left the samurai sword for her to do the number on me, and had briefed her on how to do it swiftly and efficiently.

Unfortunately for her side, my arrangements to pick her up made it impossible for her to bring along the sword. She'd sneaked out after I was asleep, taken my rented Toyota to her parked Buick, driven to her apartment for the sword, then returned in the same manner.

"I've been back an hour," she said, starting to sob again. "I've been standing in the dark, shaking, unable to do what the Sons demanded. Then I thought of my parents, my family, and I knew I must try. But I've failed. Now all my relatives will go to their ancestors in the name of the emperor."

"Not necessarily," I said. "Look, in a few days, I hope to put a stop to most of this foolishness. I can at least buy you some time."

"Buy time?"

"You wait here. I have a plan."

I went down to the hotel kitchen and rummaged around for a few items I figured to use in the plan. In a large walk-in refrigerator, I found the main item—a recently butchered but not skinned goat. I dumped the goat into a wicker basket and rummaged for more items. I found chunks of pork and beef, added them to the basket.

In another cooler, I found the most important ingredient: a huge jar of duck blood used to make soup. It's a Japanese delicacy, especially for hunters. Duck-blood soup has even gained popularity among American hunters.

It took two trips to haul the necessary items up to the room. I used pillows to fill in the missing areas of a human body under the covers. Kiko stared with wide eyes and open mouth as I prepared the "corpse."

In twenty minutes, I'd produced a special effect in the bed that truly looked as though the girl had gone into an insane frenzy and had hacked her victim up so badly that he was unrecognizable.

Kiko almost vomited when I smeared duck blood on her hands, face and clothing. I kept some back to splatter around the bed, on the walls, and, of course, to liberally cover the samurai sword.

"All right," I said, washing up in the bathroom. "You go down to the lobby, just like that. Touch railings and banisters and walls. Make a bloody mess of the phone when you call the number the Sons gave you. Tell them the job is done. They can come and inspect anytime they want."

I knew they'd be right over. They might, in fact, be waiting right downstairs. But I had the feeling that, for once, I'd tricked them enough that they had no idea where I was. They were depending on Kiko to come through for them.

In a way, she had.

"You'll have to stay here while they check out the corpse," I told the still-shocked girl. "They won't look too closely or go probing in that bloody mess. You'll be safe. Tell them you lost your temper, knowing I was an enemy of the emperor, and couldn't help yourself. Tell them you'll have your brothers dispose of the body. I think they'll be happy to pass on this one. And then get hold of your brothers and get rid of this mess before the hotel calls in the authorities. Can you do all that?"

She nodded, her eyes still riveted to the bloody thing I'd created in the bed.

"Then go," I said. "I'll stay out of sight as much as possible. Even if they do find out I'm alive, you have an out. Just say you were convinced that I was the one in the bed. Say I must have tricked you, put someone there in my place. They might believe you."

And then I sent her below to make the phone call, wondering if perhaps I'd just signed *her* death warrant.

Just in case the Sons had this hotel staked out, I took the backstairs down, went outside and circled around to watch the front from a block away. I had the .45 tucked in my belt, the eight-inch hunting knife strapped in its sheath to my left wrist, under my jacket.

They weren't long in coming. Five minutes at the most. I watched from a block away as a long Cadillac limousine eased up to the curbing in front of the hotel. Three men got out, looked up and down the empty street and slid on black hoods.

While they were inside, I decided to get closer. There was no way I could follow them at this time of night, with the streets nearly empty. The Toyota would stick out like a sore thumb.

The longer they were inside, the more worried I became about Kiko Shoshoni. Had one of the men actually had the guts to pull back the covers and see the hunks of meat and bunched pillows beneath? Had one of them turned over the blood-soaked head of the goat to see that it was not really the back of a man's head?

The answer to my question came as I was moving up closer to the Cadillac to get a better view of the three men when they emerged from the lobby. The door to the hotel opened and one man came out. He took off his black hood and leaned against the side of the building. Even from fifty feet away, hiding in the shadowed doorway of a florist's shop, I could see that his face was chalk white.

A second man came out, ran to the curbing behind the Caddy, ripped off his hood and vomited in the street. The third man strode out coolly, looked at the other two, took off his hood and went directly to the car. He opened the door and the interior light spilled all over his grim little face.

There was no mistaking it.

The third man was Nato Nakuma.

The factory manager and actual head of the Porfiro Toy Company.

A whole lot of theory turned to fact in that moment.

I knew the worst.

But, before I blew the plan to hell, I had to find out just where Nashima stood.

I don't know why it was important to determine that. It just was.

FOURTEEN

It was so quiet in the residential neighborhood that the engine of the Toyota sounded like a bunch of kindergarteners whamming away on pots and pans. I drove slowly, but that only seemed to aggravate the condition.

A quarter of a mile away from the Porfiro mansion, I parked and cut the engine and headlights. The early morning calm was almost deafening, until a nightingale broke the silence with a warm, delightful note.

I scaled the wall in the same place I'd scaled it before. This time was different, though. Every muscle and every vital organ in my body objected. Thirst was driving me half nuts and I knew it was the fever, the poison leaking from my damaged kidneys. At the pace I was going, I wouldn't last long enough to put a monkey wrench into the violent, sickening plans of Nato Nakuma and his Sons of August Six.

I decided against trying to sneak into the house. If one of those huge, burly servants caught me, he wouldn't ask questions.

I pulled the chain and the six-note melody inside went wild, mocking the nightingale. The
nightingale heard it and responded from a distance. I stepped back into the shadow of a Gingko
tree, just in case the wrong face showed up at the
door.

The face of the smiling man-servant, the one
who'd carried me to the Lincoln limo and into the
hospital, opened the door. I stepped forward,
smiled broadly.

"Ohio," I said. "Mr. Holmes to see Lady
Porfiro."

He stared at me for a long moment and I steeled
myself for an attack. I didn't want to shoot this
man, but I would. I had no chance at all in hand-
to-hand combat. The .45 was gripped in my hand,
nestled up against my right hip. I still hadn't fired
the damned thing, didn't even know if it would
fire.

"Ah," the smiling giant exploded, following
with a long stream of Japanese. He bowed, and
kept bowing, stepping aside to let me into the
house, as though it were not uncommon for battered Americans to come calling on genteel Japanese ladies at four in the morning.

Nashima was downstairs in the big living room
when the smiling man led me inside. She was not
smiling. She stood in a silk negligee, looking
haughty and imperious. Her arms were crossed beneath her ample bosom—not in the expectant,
waiting, servile gesture of the Japanese housewife,
but in the hostile, accusing, rolling-pin-attitude of

the angry American housewife.

"I suppose you have come here to die in my house," she said, her voice cold.

"Okay, so you're angry because I skipped out of the hospital. After you learn what I've discovered, you'll agree it was worth it. So, get over your anger, sit down and listen."

"After you learn what *I* have discovered," she said coolly, eyeing me with slightly diluted anger as I collapsed into one of the Western-style armchairs, "you will not be so cocksure of yourself. I spoke with the doctor yesterday. He said if you are not back in the hospital within twenty-four hours, it will be too late to keep the poison from killing you. It will be a slow and painful death."

I sat forward in the chair, touched my fingertips together, pursed my lips.

"All right. I still have some time. Sit and listen, then we'll make a quick trip to the hospital."

She sat opposite me, her back still rigid, her arms still folded beneath her breasts, her attitude still imperious, angry. Softened anger, though.

I told her of my escapades, of how hooded men had located me at the cheap hotel, how I'd gone to Kiko Shoshoni for help, how the Sons had already gotten to her. My description of the corpse ruse to throw off the Sons made her skin go whiter, but she withstood the gory description admirably. I told her of my calls to Tumio and the dark cloud passed behind her eyes. I told of his cryptic response to my question. She didn't even blink.

"All right," I said, still trying the shock effect

on her. "How's this for the capper? I recognized one of the three hooded men who came to inspect my corpse. I saw him as plainly as I'm seeing you now. He was Nato Nakuma, your esteemed factory manager, the real head of the Porfiro Toy Company."

Her body gave a slight tremor. She was holding herself upright and steady by the strongest of wills. I waited, letting shock and willpower fight it out in her lovely body. Shock won.

Like Kiko, the lovely woman collapsed in tears. Her slender hands went up to her face and she bent her head over, letting the sobs come. I waited, wanting to go and comfort her, but knowing that it would be the wrong move. I had to keep the pressure on or I'd never get the truth out of this lady.

"You should have stayed in the hospital," she cried through her hands. "You should have gone back to America. Now that you've seen one of the Sons, now that you know his name, your life is worthless. And my life is worthless."

"From what I've seen," I said a bit coldly, "except for the fact that you're very beautiful and live a really plush existence here in this mansion, your life hasn't been worth a hell of a lot. Not in the honorable sense, anyway."

She put down her hands and stared at me. "That was a cruel thing to say."

"Truth is rarely anything but cruel. In spite of that, we need a lot more of it around here. Suppose you try some of it yourself and tell me the whole story, the real story."

There were things she honestly didn't know. But what she was able to tell me—and it was plenty—was enough to lend greater credence to my theory.

The Sons of August Six, she said, had been in control of the toy company for years. In April, she said, three hooded men came to her house and told her she was to keep to her office and stay out of factory operations. She wasn't even to attend board meetings or see reports on products or production. A new toy was to be introduced late in the year, hopefully in time for Christmas. One of the factory's engineers had been given the task of inventing that toy, based on an idea one of the Sons had.

To make their orders stick, certain parts of the factory were made off limits to Nashima. Off limits, in fact, to anyone not cleared personally by Nato Nakuma.

"I was to keep all this to myself," she said. "If I did not, I would be killed, along with my father and my brothers. The Sons would seek out all other relatives until my entire bloodline was gone. I had no choice but to go along."

I caught the bit about the "brothers," but decided to let it slide, for now. There were more important fish to catch.

"Did you have any idea what this new toy was, or what the Sons might have in mind?"

"None. I knew, of course, that the Sons of August Six are interested only in revenge upon America and its Allies who fought against Japan during the war. I knew that all this had something to do with revenge."

"Yeah," I said, feeling a chill as my theory seemed more and more to be fact. "Something to do with revenge. Yet, in spite of this threat on your life and your bloodline, you called David Hawk. Why?"

"A faint hope," she said thinly. "A straw to the drowning person. After the explosion in one of the packing rooms, I suspected that the revenge would take the form of violent death, perhaps on a wide scale. I thought if David Hawk came, pretending to be a toy salesman, made discreet inquiries and investigation, he might find a way to help, to stop them. But you came, they knew who you were—or that you weren't a toy salesman—and everything went wrong. My father, my brother and I have been threatened many times since you came."

"Earlier, you said you would be killed along with your father and your brothers," I said, watching her face closely for reaction. "Now, you mention only your father and your brother. Do you have more than one brother?"

"No," she said quickly, too quickly. "Just one brother. If I said 'brothers,' it was a slip of the tongue."

"Yeah." I remained silent, watching her. The damned woman was still lying. Or, at least, leaving something out. I took a long shot.

"How about Tumio? Is he under threat?"

She looked up, failing to conceal a gasp. "I—I really can't say. I don't know."

She was stammering all over the place. I

stopped her. "Can this Tumio really be trusted?"

"Oh yes, yes, of course. Implicitly."

I was getting hot there, but decided to leave it for another time. If Tumio was a brother, I'd know about it soon enough. And it really had little to do with the real issues here. I just didn't like the idea of this lady lying or holding out. I took another tack.

"Did you know that the toy robot, Tikki-Tik, will sell in the United States and other countries for as little as forty dollars?"

She sat bolt upright. "How did you learn this?"

"From Tumio."

"Then they have reached him," she said, her pretty face going sad. "You forced him into giving a figure and they instructed him to give the wrong figure. The robot will sell for much less. Only ten dollars."

I whistled. Jesus, at that price, I'd buy a few thousand and peddle them myself.

"Do you know how much each toy costs your company to produce?"

"Not exactly," she said. "But a member of the board who resists what the Sons are doing has contacted me. He is concerned about bankruptcy. I would guess that our cost is more than two hundred dollars for each toy."

"That's one hell of a markdown. The company can't help but go bankrupt."

She began to wring her hands. "What can I do? What can anyone do to keep us from going bankrupt?"

I didn't tell her my theory of why the Sons were forcing the company to make a toy that cost two hundred dollars and to sell it for ten. I think she had an idea that it was pretty grim, but the fact of it might blow her mind, make her useless to my plan.

"There's still another problem to be resolved before I ask you a big favor," I said, shifting in the seat to give a throbbing kidney more space. "There's a leak somewhere. Someone you must have told about your call to Hawk leaked the word to the Sons. That's the only explanation as to how my cover was blown even before I got here."

"I told no one," she said.

"You had to tell Tumio something. He met me in Tokyo, gave me weapons. Hawk was in direct touch with him."

"I told him only that a friend might come to help me check on the explosion. I told him nothing of the threat from the Sons of August Six. I've told him nothing of my nominal ranking at the company. I put him in touch with Hawk so that he could facilitate matters in Tokyo, knowing that Hawk could not carry weapons on the plane unless he used his government status as leverage. That, alone, could have tipped off the Sons."

"As it turned out," I said bitterly, "they were tipped off anyway. Unless I find out who's responsible, any plans I make will be doomed to failure before I get them off the ground."

"I told them," a heavy, thick voice said from the background.

Nashima and I both turned. A young man with

a large head and thick lips stood at the entrance to the room. He was wearing a traditional Japanese toga. His jet black hair and slanted black eyes marked him as Japanese. He looked like a young, coarse-featured Nashima. I knew he was her retarded brother.

"Nariko," she said. "Please return to your room and let the gentleman and I converse. This does not concern you."

"Yes it does," the boy said in pretty fair English. "I've been listening. I know what you're talking about. They have talked to me many times."

"Who has talked to you, Nariko?" Nashima asked. Her voice was soft, motherly.

"The men in the black hoods. They have talked to me and I have talked to them. I told them about you calling the man from America."

Nashima's voice took on a note of anguish. "But, Nariko, how did you know I called anyone in America?"

"You wrote it in your book," the boy said. "I can read, you know. I read the book."

Nashima's face went white again. She sagged in the chair. "My God, I'd forgotten about my diary. I've been putting everything down since the first threat came. I'd arranged to give the diary to my attorneys in case anything happened to me or anyone in my family."

The relief that washed over me was almost visible. I had mistrusted Nashima and still hadn't begun to trust her completely. I was dead certain she had told someone—her brother, her father, *some-one* and was lying to me. But she hadn't been lying. A retarded brother, not nearly as retarded as Nashima thought, had inadvertently blown my cover.

"Did I do right, Nashima?" Nariko asked, cocking his head with puzzlement, seeking approbation.

"You did fine, Nariko. Now, ask Toko to give you a glass of milk, then return to bed. You need your sleep."

When he was gone, we just stared at each other.

I was relieved, but the feeling was short-lived. As I sat there gazing at the lovely Nashima Porfiro, grateful that at least one mystery had been cleared up, I began to feel peculiar. My head began to spin, my kidneys to throb. But I couldn't crash now. I had to learn the truth about Tumio.

"Tell me about your other brother," I said weakly, feeling the dizziness grow. "Tell me about Tumio. He must resemble your father and that's why I didn't . . ."

I had this strange sensation of falling, of violent movement. I saw Nashima's face loom large in my sight. Felt myself fall into her arms.

The poison was working faster than the doctors had thought it would.

I remember the softness and fragrance of her, and then I was out cold.

FIFTEEN

Once again, I found myself rigged to IV bottles, with Nashima sitting in the chair beside my hospital bed. I welcomed the painkillers, though my body was responding nicely after the beating it had taken. Kiko's tender ministrations had helped in that department.

In spite of the drugs, I was acutely conscious of the passing time. That ship, the *Endiro Gotsu,* would be leaving in two days and I was flat on my back. It would do no good to call Hawk, especially with only a theory to go on. Even if I had proof, I knew what Hawk's response would be.

"You were sent to Hiroshima to solve the problem. So solve it."

I still hadn't revealed my theory to Nashima. I didn't want to, not until I had some bit of physical evidence to support it. My plan to get that evidence was being thwarted by this damned kidney problem.

Finally, in the middle of the afternoon, more

than thirty hours after I'd collapsed, I sat up in bed, determined to act.

"What do you think you're doing?" Nashima demanded.

"I'm going out to buy something," I said. "Get the nurse in here to remove this damned IV."

"Nick, you can't," she said, coming to the bedside, putting her hands on my shoulders. So soft, those hands. Her eyes sought mine, pleaded. "What is it you want to buy. Perhaps I can get it for you."

"I want a piece of black cloth," I said. "I want to make a hood out of it."

Her hands tightened on my shoulders.

"You must not make terrible jokes," she said.

"No joke. I've finally figured a way to get into that damned warehouse, that packing room. Nobody ever questions these black-hooded thugs as they move about the country threatening and killing. I've seen those guards at the factory. They're kids. I imagine they'd shake in their boots if one of the Sons showed up."

"Probably," she said, "but you can't do it. You have to wait at least another twenty-four hours. You have to—"

"I have to follow my hunches, prove my theory," I cut her off. "I have a hunch that things are moving faster than I'd thought. I have a hunch that I may already be too late."

"What is this hunch, this theory?"

All right. She'd been honest and open with me,

finally. The least I could do was be honest and open with her.

I told her my theory for what I knew intuitively was being planned by the Sons of August Six. Her face grew progressively whiter as I talked. At the end, her body sagged, believing, then she shored up her body, stiffening in front of me.

"Give me a couple of hours," she said. She picked up her purse and nodded to Toko who was smiling off in a corner of the room.

"Hey, don't go off half-cocked," I said. "You can't bring in the authorities on just a theory."

"We can't ever bring in the authorities," she said. "Their ranks are riddled with the black-hooded ones. First, I must talk with the doctor to see if you can be given an antibiotic that will work for the next several hours. Next, I must—well, let it be a surprise."

Two hours later, she was back, her face bright, her eyes glittering. She was wearing her jade again and, as we walked from the hospital, the sunlight caught in it, making it glitter brightly.

"What's the surprise?" I asked as Toko held the door for us and helped us into the big Lincoln.

"You'll see."

Once the car was a part of the whizzing, whirling, horn-blowing Hiroshima traffic, Nashima opened her purse and took out two black hoods, complete with eyeholes.

"Try this on," she said. "I had to guess at the size."

As I stared at the ugly hood, Nashima put the

other one over her head. Her eyes sparkled at me through the little slanted holes.

"No," I said, guessing her plan. "You're not going with me."

"It is my factory," she said. "It is time I did the honorable thing and became an active part of its operations." She giggled beneath the hood, like a teenager. "Even if I do have to sneak in like a bandit."

As I parked the Honda I'd rented, Nashima Porfiro clutched her purse and stared at the darkened factory ahead. I was grateful that Nato Nakuma hadn't yet started extra shifts. The place was shut down, with only those rube-looking guards walking around the place with oversized guns.

I had the untried .45 in my back pocket, the hunting knife strapped to my left wrist. Nashima had a small .32 caliber Colt automatic she kept at home for protection against prowlers.

Every instinct in me told me that I should go this alone, that it was no place for a soft person like Nashima. But she'd been adamant about coming. Maybe she wasn't as soft as I thought.

"All right, listen up," I said as I shut off the engine and turned in the seat to face her. "We go over the fence behind the warehouse, but our first target is the packing room. The one for toys being shipped to the United States. To get there, we have to walk through some guards. We do it with the hoods on, but we walk boldly and purposefully, as though we're on some kind of important mission."

"That will be easy to do," she replied. "The mission *is* important."

"I don't mean it that way. I mean, important to the Sons of August Six. We have to be bold and maybe a little brutal. If a guard tries to stop us, bark an order in Japanese for him to get out of our way. Use the emperor gimmick. We're on an errand for the emperor. If that doesn't work, you keep the guard busy while I go to work with the knife. The guns are not to be used unless we're in mortal danger."

She smiled, that old rueful smile. "To tell you the truth, Nick, I'd rather we didn't even use the knife."

"We'll do what we have to do. No more. No less. Either we agree on that or we don't go in."

"We agree on that."

She agreed, but I knew her heart wasn't in it. Not the taking of human life. She felt sorry for the young men who'd been called in as guards. She said they were trainees for the Sons of August Six, and she knew about such trainees. They were conscripted from threatened families, brainwashed, put through rigorous training and finally tested under life-survival stress before they earned their black hoods.

The young men had no option of turning back, of resigning. Resignation or failure to carry out an assignment meant death to them and to all of their bloodline.

I felt sorry for them, too, but I'd kill one in a

split second if I thought he'd blow our mission tonight. I had to make certain Nashima realized that
and was properly impressed with the importance of
such a harsh stand.

"Let's go."

I opened the door and went around to her side
of the car. She was already on the sidewalk, the
black hood clutched in her hand. We walked
soundlessly, virtually tiptoeing through an open
field toward the rear of the factory compound.

When we reached the spot where the barbed
wire was slack, I boosted Nashima up. When my
hands touched those nicely rounded buttocks, I
felt a tingle. It was incredible that this middle-
aged woman could work the magic of the adolescent on me. But the tingle was undeniably there.
Someday, somewhere, I would have to find out
just how far the magic went.

When I dropped down into the factory yard,
Nashima already had her hood in place. The sight
gave me a start, then I saw those sparkling eyes. I
smiled at her and put on my own hood. The smile
died instantly; I felt trapped in the hood. I also
felt evil, as though I could get away with anything
I wanted with total impunity. It is that human reaction to masks and hoods, I suppose, that makes
gangs like the Sons of August Six and the Ku Klux
Klan effective.

We checked the warehouse first. The doors were
locked, but we could see through the dirty windows
that the warehouse was nearly full of the big
wooden crates, ready for shipping. Now, we had to

get into the shipping room itself, to prove or dis-
prove my theory. I motioned to Nashima, nod-
ding toward the corner of the building.

"Stay behind me," I whispered through the
cloth. "If we encounter a guard, I'll bow and
keep on going. If we're challenged, you start talking while I circle behind him."

She nodded. Her eyes lost some sparkle as fear
began to set in. The danger of our little job of simple burglary hadn't reached her until we were actually at it. Now, I knew, fear was coursing through
her veins like adrenaline through an athlete's
muscles.

I moved out ahead, striding around the warehouse as though I owned the place, lock, stock
and barrel. I saw guards far to the left, along the
side fence. They looked our way, saw the black
hoods and quickly looked away, as though in the
presence of the emperor. Even so, I could tell that
they were sneaking sidelong peeks at us.

I set a bearing for the section Kiko had told me
was the new wing for packing robots for shipment
to the United States. I knew the doors would be
locked, but that was the beautiful part of my plan.
I also knew that Nashima had keys for those
doors, keys she hadn't used since the Sons of August Six had entered the picture. They hadn't
thought to take the keys; I just hoped they hadn't
thought to change the locks on the doors.

They hadn't. As I watched the guards, a bit sur-
reptitiously, Nashima got out her keys and opened
the door to the office where Nato Nakuma and his
friends had held their meeting during my last un-

happy visit here. The key turned and she pushed inside, knowing precisely where she was going.

I took a last look around the compound, saw that the guards were studiously pretending they hadn't seen us, and closed the door. Nashima snapped on a ceiling light while I pulled the shade.

I checked my chronometer then. I'd calculated that the turning on of that light would trigger a call to Nato Nakuma at his home. At least one of the guards would be on orders to keep the boss posted of all activity at the factory.

At best, I figured, we had twenty minutes to check the two sites I'd chosen as vital and get back over that fence. We'd save some time not having to retrace our steps. We'd end up in the warehouse, so it would be a simple matter to exit through a rear door and, voilá, there would be the fence.

"This way," Nashima said, her voice strangely muffled by the black cloth. "I haven't been here since the changeover, but I don't imagine they've altered the building's structure."

We went into a dark corridor, then into a large room with several huge tables and a conveyor belt. Nashima turned on the light in there. The tables were loaded with completed robots. Beside each table were wooden crates and small boxes. The packers put the robots into the boxes, then the boxes into the crates. A forklift truck, standing idly by, obviously hoisted the crates onto the conveyor.

The conveyor led to a closed metal door, much like a huge overhead garage door. I reasoned that the crates were taken off during operations and loaded aboard special transports to haul them to the warehouse, fifty yards across the compound. It would have been more efficient to have the warehouse directly attached to the wing, but this was an old factory, built in a less efficient time.

I picked up one of the robots and was surprised at its lightness. It couldn't have weighed more than nine or ten pounds. Yet, Nato Nakuma had said each Tikki-Tik weighed about twenty pounds, without batteries. I looked around for a scale, and my eye fell on a door that had been reinforced with wide metal bands.

"Do you have a key to that room?" I asked Nashima.

She looked toward the door, and shook her head. "I've never seen that door," she said. "The room behind it should be a large storage area, but there was an ordinary door when I was last here."

I checked the door; it was locked. I knelt to the floor, ran my finger across the boards and smelled by fingers. Nothing.

"What are you looking for?" Nashima asked.

"It doesn't matter," I said. "What I expected isn't here."

I walked around the room, aware that time was leaking away, that I'd learned only one tiny fact that might or might not mean anything. The robots were half the weight that Nato had indicated. I had a thought.

I went to the big wooden crates and found one that hadn't been sealed. It wasn't quite full of the small boxes that held the robots. I reached in with one hand to lift one out, to check it.

My fingers slipped off the box, it was so heavy. I tugged with both hands, finally had to get a purchase on the bottom to bring out the box.

"That's more like it," I said. "I'd guess close to twenty pounds."

"Perhaps they put something in the bottom of the box to make it weigh more."

"With today's shipping costs, they'd more likely put something in to make it weigh less. Like helium, perhaps."

I broke the seal on the box and lifted out the robot. Nothing in the box. The weight was all in the toy. I looked at Nashima, but she couldn't tell that I was grimacing under my hood.

My theory was almost proven fact.

I opened a drawer and there were six Phillip's head screwdrivers inside. I picked one up and was just removing the first of eight screws when we heard footsteps, and saw the young guard in the open doorway.

He said something in Japanese. He seemed embarrassed to be in our presence. I waited.

"He said he called the factory manager and learned that we aren't supposed to be here tonight," Nashima whispered to me. "He says nobody is to touch the toys. What do I tell him?"

I watched the young guard, saw him shift about anxiously, awkwardly. His rifle was resting on the floor, but the way his knuckles were white, I knew that he was ready to hoist it into action if he didn't get the right response.

"Tell him that I'm a special inspector from the

emperor's office," I whispered. "Tell him that I've found something drastically wrong and he's to come and see for himself."

Her body sagged. She knew I would kill the guard when he came near. In fact, I was already snaking my hand around to take the hunting knife out of its sheath.

Nashima spoke harshly in Japanese. At least, it sounded harsh. The guard snapped to attention. His face paled. He saluted us, picked up his weapon, turned on his heel and marched out of the place. We heard the office door open and close.

"It's all right," Nashima said. "He's gone."

"What the hell did you say to him?"

"I hope I turned the tables on Nato Nakuma," she said. "I told him that you were indeed the emperor's special inspector, and that something was wrong, but I didn't ask him to come near. I didn't want to see him killed by you."

"How did you get him to leave like that?"

"I told him that the emperor was unhappy with the factory manager, had relieved him of duty. I told him to detain the manager if he should come here. Did I buy us some time?"

"You sure as hell did," I said, "but you won't save the guard's life. As soon as Nato tumbles, he'll have the kid killed."

"I know," she said sadly. "But I won't have to witness it."

She was some woman, Nashima Porfiro. I gazed at her with renewed interest. She wasn't nearly as soft as I'd thought. Squeamish about death, maybe, but hardly soft. In a pinch, she'd do fine.

In twenty seconds, I had the panel off the robot.

And there it was, the proof that my theory was fact.

Under those black hoods, both our faces went immediately white.

SIXTEEN

"Nick, we must go," Nashima reminded me. "Our twenty minutes are almost up."

I was deliberately but not so calmly removing the plastic-covered packet from the belly of the robot. Sweat was trickling down my neck and sides. My hands on the packet were clammy.

"Just another minute," I said. "My theory has proven true, but I don't have all the facts. There must be a timer in here, somewhere."

Nashima went to the window, pulled the shade aside and looked out. I could sense her fear and nervousness in her body movements. And her eyes when she looked back from the window.

"The guards have gathered in a group," she said. "They're watching this window."

"Let them," I said. "I have to find out if there's a timer."

The plan of the Sons of August Six was simple and grisly. The sophisticated robots would sell for a fraction of what they were really worth. At ten bucks a crack, every kid in America would want one—and would get it.

There was one catch. Stashed in the belly of each

Tikki-Tik was a ten-pound packet of TNT or dynamite. I doubted if they'd use cordite—low explosives were too easily sniffed out by the trained dogs used by U.S. Customs, and would not give nearly the punch of high explosives like TNT or dynamite.

One ten-pound packet of high explosives would blow the average American house clear off the map, along with the family inside it.

And these people were planning to ship nearly two million of these packets to America, inside the bellies of harmless-looking toy robots.

The implications were more than grisly. They made the detonation of the first A-bomb and its consequent snuffing out of seventy-five thousand lives look inconsequential by comparison.

Death and desolation would range from the Atlantic to the Pacific, instead of being confined to one city.

My guess was that the high explosive in the belly of this robot was set to go off sometime on Christmas day.

One gigantic Christmas kill.

All in retribution for an act of war that had ended more than thirty-five years ago.

Revenge, I knew, was another of man's obsessions, though hardly secret. But revenge of this magnitude after more than thirty-five years? It was incredible, unbelievable.

And yet the proof of it was right in my hands, right before my eyes.

"Nick, someone has arrived at the gate. I see headlights."

I found the timer and began to study the dial. Sweat poured into my palms, made me almost drop the packet of explosives.

"What are the guards doing?" I asked in a tight, anxious voice.

"Flocking to the gate," she said.

"Good. Your quick thinking with that guard has given me a couple of extra minutes. I won't need half that."

The dial of the timer was set in days. The number opposite a tiny arrow was twenty-eight. I made a quick calculation of days. Yes, the explosives would go off on Christmas.

The timer made no ticking sound, so I guessed that it was run electronically, by a tiny computer chip battery embedded inside. I thought of resetting the timer to the number two, hoping to foil the plan that way. When this little bugger went off two days hence, in the warehouse, it would take the whole batch of robots with it.

Along with another large section of Hiroshima.

While I was battling with that moral decision, Nashima turned from the window and ran toward me, her pistol drawn.

"They're heading this way," she said. "My orders apparently didn't hold up. Nato Nakuma is coming with the guards."

I didn't bother to put the toy back together. No time. I gathered up the various parts, shoved the empty box back into the crate and motioned for Nashima to cut the lights.

"Is there a back way out or do we have to go through that little office again?"

She led the way, I followed. We were at a back door, looking out on the warehouse, when we heard the office door open with a bang. Nato was madder than a hornet, coming our way.

We dashed across to the warehouse, circled it and found the spot where we'd climbed the fence. Fortunately, Nato had all the guards with him. They were still searching the wing of the factory.

I took a few seconds to put the robot together again, boosted Nashima up and quickly followed. Three minutes later, we were in the rented Honda, tooling away northward. We crossed twenty bridges before my pulse began to return to normal.

"That was close," Nashima said, her breath exploding against the cold windshield. "My God, that was close."

"You keep saying, 'my God,'" I said. "Shouldn't you be saying something about Buddha?"

"I am a Christian," she said. "My whole family is Christian."

"I see. Well, it's a good thing, maybe."

"What a strange thing to say," she said.

"Not so strange when you consider that we can't go back to your house now. Nato will know that you were with me tonight. The guard knows you're a woman."

"So? There are many women among the Sons of August Six."

"Yeah, but how many of them have keys to various doors at the factory?"

"I see. Where do you propose that we go?"

"To the home of some good Christian," I said.

"A friend. Someone you can trust with your life. With all our lives."

"You mean, both our lives."

"No, all our lives. We'll pick up your father and brother, then swing by and pick up Kiko Shoshoni."

"Why will you pick up Kiko?"

"Because I've signed her death warrant as well. After tonight, they'll know she didn't kill me in that hotel room. And they'll be so angry that we sneaked into the place and learned their secret, they won't accept her alibi that she thought she'd killed the right man."

"How will they know that we learned the secret? You put the box back in the crate. They'll never miss the robot."

"I'm afraid they will," I said, glancing down at the silent little mechanical man on the seat between us. "When they weigh that crate and find it twenty pounds lighter than the others, they'll know. And they'll have to weigh the crate for the shipping manifest."

"How do you know all these things?"

"Spies know everything," I said, grinning at her to show that I was joking.

Her return smile was serious. "I believe you. And I know just the place for us to go."

"Then let's not waste any time."

I speeded up the little Honda, racing into another unknown.

Were we heading for another sanctuary, or another trap?

SEVENTEEN

It was a sanctuary, in the strictest sense of the word.

It was the Christian Youth Home of the church where Nashima's family had gone for two generations.

Carl and Joan Jordan, the missionaries who had started the youth house, accepted us without question. They even drove the Honda and Kiko Shoshoni's battered Buick into the church garage to get them out of sight.

"How long will you be our guests?" was the only question Carl asked.

"Not long," I said. "I just want to keep these people safe while I make a couple of contacts. We should be out of your hair in a day or so."

"You are welcome for as long as you have need," he said. His smile was genuine, as was his desire to help. I liked the guy, even though I felt uncomfortable in his presence. Ministers and missionaries always affect me that way. I suppose it's the same with all sinners.

The Christian Youth Home was on one of the middle islands, not far from the downtown section. Carl said I could use one of the mission's cars if I liked. I appreciated that. It wouldn't do to have Kiko's Buick or my rented vehicle on the streets. The Sons would be looking for those cars.

Kiko and Nashima settled in the main bedroom of the big, rambling house. Nashima's father and brother shared another bedroom and I slept in a small barracks-like room. We'd come at a good time—the children who normally used the home were off on a junket to Tokyo. Carl and Joan would go there in three days to pick them up.

By then, we'd be long gone. The ship sailed in two days.

After our hosts left us, and Nashima's father and brother had gone to sleep, I knocked on the master bedroom door, then went in.

Nashima and Kiko were sitting on the bed, talking. They spoke in Japanese, but I knew that Nashima was telling the girl about our little breaking and entering gig.

"We have to make plans," I said. "We're in trouble. My guess is that they'll turn up every rock and jar-lid in the city to find us. They'll also speed up the departure of the ship if they can. Not only do we have to keep out of the way of their samurai swords and bombs, we have to find a way to stop that ship from leaving."

"Big problems," Nashima said. "Do you have any ideas?"

"The most obvious one is to make contact with

David Hawk and lay it all out for him. The only trouble is, I know what his answer will be. He'll tell me to handle it myself."

Nashima pursed her lips in thought. Her face brightened, then darkened, then brightened again.

"We must forget the ship," she said. "We must make certain those things do not leave the warehouse."

"Good thinking," I said, trying not to sound sarcastic. "And just how do you propose doing that with the formidable forces we have."

Our "forces" were hardly formidable. I was running out of steam again. Nashima had admitted that she'd never fired the pistol she had. Kiko was too young and inexperienced to program for complicated action, Nashima's father was ancient and doddering and her brother was mentally out of it.

"I have a very large family," Nashima said cryptically. "Oh, I'm not thinking of my father and Nariko, and that we can no longer trust Tumio. I am talking about my bloodline, the ones that would be killed by the Sons of August Six if I step out of line."

It was the first time she'd admitted that Tumio was her brother, or that we could no longer trust him. Anxious as I was to learn about the peculiar arrangement between her and Tumio, I decided once again to postpone discussion of it.

"What makes you think your relatives will do anything that might put them in danger?" I asked.

"They are already in danger," she said. "I have stepped out of line. At dawn, I will start the calls, gather the clan together. We shall form an army and invade that warehouse."

I sighed. It was a hare-brained scheme at best. But it was the only scheme in town. But I had to try an alternative, any alternative.

"I really think we should call in the police. The proof is right out there in that warehouse, even though a few truckloads have already been taken to the ship."

"And the police ranks are filled with men from the Sons of August Six. I thought spies knew everything."

"I know you told me that," I said. "I also know that any terrorist organization likes to spread the word that they've infiltrated the ranks of the authorities. It's a most effective way of keeping victims in line."

"Can we take the chance that the Sons have lied, that they aren't among the ranks of the police?"

I sighed again.

And slept uneasily, alone.

Shortly before first light, I felt pressure on the side of the bed. My hand tightened on the .45 under my pillow. My body was already steeled for an attack when I opened my eyes and I saw Nashima, naked, leaning over me. Her hands were on the mattress.

"Pardon my forwardness," she said, "but I cannot keep back my feelings any longer. If you do not find this old woman undesirable, I should like to join your bed."

Jesus, I could hardly believe my eyes. She was

exquisite, the most desirable creature I'd seen in years.

I threw back the covers and opened my arms to her. She smiled, her eyes sparkled and she came into my bed.

What followed was a deep experience of heated passion that seemed to go on and on through eternity. The softness of her, the fragrance of her, the tenderness of her—these were the high points of a physical and emotional high that blossomed and exploded in that narrow bed in that long room in that fine Christian home.

When Nashima left my bed an hour later, I had no recall of fleshly details. The memory was a total one, of passion, of satisfaction, of fulfillment.

And I was exhausted. Pleasantly so.

EIGHTEEN

They began arriving at noon. Some came in kimonos and togas, some in Western-style garb. If they had weapons, they kept them well concealed.

Carl and Joan welcomed them all, inviting them to sit at the big table in the kitchen where Joan, Nashima and Kiko had prepared an enormous meal.

Nashima had spent the morning in the telephone booth down at the corner. I spent the morning outside the booth, keeping watch, looking for anyone who might be interested in what we were doing.

What magic words she'd used on these distant relatives, I didn't know, but they had worked.

By one o'clock, we had an army of a hundred people, ranging in age from great uncles at seventy to third cousins of fourteen. Some were rich, most were poor. At best, though, they represented a rag-tag army of frightened, unprepared, untrained and undisciplined children. But they had one thing on their side: They'd suffered long enough under the threat of the Sons of August Six and were determined to remove that threat, or die in the effort.

If determination counted for anything, Nato Nakuma and his Sons had better keep close watch on their toys.

In the afternoon, Carl and Joan left on errands. I assembled the relatives of Nashima Porfiro—representing nearly all the males in the bloodline—in the kitchen and conducted weapons inspection. Most of them had knives and swords, but some had guns. Good guns, respectable guns. One nephew even had a Luger that looked so much like Wilhelmina that I wanted to confiscate it for myself.

Five had rifles strapped to their bodies under their togas. They weren't new rifles, but they were in good condition. And they had plenty of ammunition.

And they had plenty of cars. Nobody can say that the Japanese of today are starving for wheels.

My plan was so simple that I was embarrassed to reveal it. But I did, with Nashima as interpreter.

We would go in a caravan to the factory, in broad daylight. I would lead in my rented Honda. I would simply crash through the gates and lead my army right up to the warehouse. If any guards resisted, we would shoot to kill.

"But no shooting unless absolutely necessary," I had Nashima tell them. "A stray bullet could hit one of those robots. The TNT in those plastic pouches will explode on impact as well as by electronic timer."

Once we had the factory in control, Nashima would call in the chief of police. Our army of relatives would make certain that the police did their jobs. We'd insist on nothing short of disarming all the toys, taking the explosives to a safe place for detonation and arresting Nato Nakuma and all the guards. It wasn't likely we could extend our tentacles farther. Even under extreme torture, Nato wouldn't reveal the names of his black-hooded friends.

I had already decided that, once the threat to American kids was removed, I'd stay in Japan to help Nashima in her battle against the Sons of August Six. I had no hopes of eliminating the terrorist group, but I would make them back off on their threats against Nashima and her relatives. Somehow.

Perhaps I'd resolved to stay as a salve to my American conscience. After all, Nashima and her people were taking this bold act to keep millions of Americans from being blown up in their homes on Christmas day. The least I could do was stay and help her with the problems that would arise in the aftermath.

Then, again, perhaps conscience had nothing to do with it. My memory of that marvelous hour of love-making was sharp. I wanted more of this lady, much more.

At three o'clock, we were as ready as we would ever be. I checked the guns again, found them all loaded, cocked and ready. I arranged for at least one man with a gun to be in each of the first several cars. The rear echelon would be made up of people with knives and swords.

I lost the battle to have Nashima and Kiko stay behind, in the sanctuary.

"We do not have women's rights here in Japan," Nashima reminded me, "but we Japanese women do have rights, in our own way. You must not be a chauvinist, Nick."

"Chauvinism has nothing to do with this," I said to Nashima. "Kiko isn't even armed and you don't even know how to fire that pistol."

"I lied to you," she said, grinning. "My husband was a marksman with every firearm available. He taught me well. I lied because I did not want you to think me unfeminine."

I was delighted about this particular "unfeminine" trait. But I couldn't resist a jab. "Now who's being chauvinist?"

"I am sorry, but at my age, a woman—"

"Is very beautiful," I said, cutting her short. I held her eyes for a moment and she knew that I was sincere. I motioned toward Kiko. "She has no weapon. She has no strength to fight in hand-to-hand combat. If it's being chauvinistic not to want her to endanger herself, then so be it."

Nashima pursed those lovely lips. Before Joan and Carl left, Joan whispered to me, "There is an old gun in the attic, left here by the former missionaries. I shall return shortly."

She hiked up her kimono and went upstairs. Soon, we heard her bumping around in the attic. She returned, dusty and covered with cobwebs. In her hands were an ancient rifle and a wooden box.

"It is old," she said, "but I think it works."

I took the rifle and could hardly believe my eyes. It was a Henry Rifle, invented in 1860 by B. T. Henry, who also invented the rimfire cartridge to go with it. In its heyday, the Henry could fire fifteen rounds of .28 caliber slugs without reloading. But it had one hell of a kick.

This rifle, I guessed, was probably made in 1880, more than a hundred years ago. I checked the hammer, ran the cocking arm back and forth, pulled the trigger on the empty chamber. It would work fine, but it would shatter Kiko's slender shoulder.

In the box were a hundred rounds of antique cartridges for the Henry. I loaded the rifle's magazine with fifteen cartridges, ran the spring home and cocked a bullet into the chamber.

"It'll work," I said, "but not for Kiko. We'll trade one of the husky cousins for something a bit more delicate."

Kiko was angry, but I had no choice. The first time she fired that antique weapon, she'd wind up on her lovely ass. The burly young cousin was delighted to have the monster rifle in exchange for a Smith & Wesson .22 caliber target pistol.

"Okay, Nashima," I said as the relatives poured outside to climb into their vehicles, "call the police chief and tell him to be at the factory with plenty of cops in thirty minutes."

She made the call and we set off in the caravan.

I drove the Honda, with Nashima in the passenger's seat. In the rear were Kiko behind me and the cousin with the Henry Rifle behind Nashima. The cousin's name was Sonito.

Twenty-five cars, pickup trucks, jeeps and limousines stretched out behind us. I'd had everyone turn on their headlights and had instructed each driver to keep the ranks closed. The plan worked, but only to a point. There were times when I couldn't spot a single vehicle behind me with headlights turned on, then suddenly they'd all be there, right in line. Where they'd been, I have no idea.

And then, about halfway to the southernmost island, other motorists responded to our headlights in a rather peculiar way. If we had on our lights, they apparently figured, there must be a good reason for it. Suddenly, every headlight in the city was going on.

In spite of my fear that this would hamper our ranks, maybe even send some of our rag-tag army following the wrong vehicles to the wrong places. I had to grin. I recalled a gag my buddies and I used to pull in high school. We'd go outside after school, as others were emerging, and gaze up at the sky as though there were something interesting up there. Within minutes, the entire student body would be staring at the sky, asking each other what the hell was up there.

As we cleared the last bridge, our army had grown to perhaps a hundred cars, all with their headlights on, their horns blowing.

"My God, Nick," Nashima cried, looking back. "They'll mess everything up. They'll warn Nato that we're coming."

"Not necessarily," I said, grinning at her.

"Sometimes, there's more profit in mass confusion than there is in tight discipline. Even if Nato is warned, he won't be able to clear out that warehouse before we get to it. We'll have our evidence and, once the confusion is sorted out, the results will be just what we seek."

"But those people are innocent, they have nothing to do with our battle. They might get killed."

"I doubt it," I said. "That's another plus. When this gang of cars comes crashing into the factory compound, I think the guards will be so terrified of our numbers, they won't fire a single shot. They'll more likely throw down their weapons."

"You can't be sure of that."

"Then, we'll load the dice," I said. "As soon as I crash through the gate, let's all start firing our weapons into the air. The relatives behind us will do the same. We'll give those guards the shock treatment."

She nodded, smiling. It would work and she knew it. We were turning what had seemed to be a gigantic negative into a wholesome positive.

The factory loomed ahead. The main gates, fortunately, were on a corner. We didn't have to make much of a turn to go directly through them. Which meant, of course, that we didn't even have to slow down.

"Get your weapons ready," I said as I pressed down on the accelerator and picked up speed. "And all windows down."

I saw the guards milling about the factory compound. They looked sleepy, bored. From behind us somewhere came the wail of police sirens. Either they were responding to Nashima's call, or they were trying to find out what the hell was going on with Hiroshima's drivers going around in broad daylight with their headlights on.

The guards ahead spotted us and began moving toward the main gate. I pushed harder on the gas pedal. The little Honda literally lurched forward. Behind me, the others were keeping pace, speeding up.

I laid on the horn and aimed the old .45 toward the sky as the nose of the Honda whammed into the gates with a screech and a yowl that could have been heard on the northernmost island.

The guards were already beginning to scatter when I cut loose with the .45. Within a fraction of a second, Nashima and Kiko popped their little guns, then the cousin, Sonito, pulled the trigger on the Henry rifle.

The boom damned near tore off the top of the Honda. I know it didn't do our eardrums any good. As for the guards, they were properly terrified. They were running full out away from us even before the people behind us began to fire their weapons.

I aimed the Honda for the vicinity of the warehouse, skirting around trucks and dock workers, blowing the horn. The long caravan behind me kept apace, accompanying the horn-blowing with battle cries that filled the air with the sound of angry bleats.

I'd been right about the guards. They had flung down their rifles and retreated to far corners of the fenced compound. Some of them even disappeared into the various wings of the factory.

"Enough shooting," I yelled as loud as I could. "We can't chance a stray bullet hitting the wrong thing and blowing us all into the river."

As soon as Nashima, Kiko and Sonito stopped firing, the relatives behind us followed suit.

I rounded the American wing of the factory and headed for the warehouse. My greatest fear now was that, when I tried to stop, all those maniacs behind me would crash into the Honda. I tapped the brakes a few times as a signal.

The whole long line of cars behind me slowed and I could imagine a hundred-plus pairs of taillights going off in perfect synchronization. At the heart of Japanese driving habits, there is an enigmatic discipline that isn't discernible to the casual observer—but it's there.

When I finally stopped and got out of the car, waving the big .45 and signaling the relatives to get out and take up posts at various doors to the factory and warehouse, police cars began to stream into the compound.

And, from the back door of the factory—the one through which Nashima and I had escaped—came a furious, red-faced little Nato Nakuma. He was chewing on a fat cigar and his angry visage reminded me of a dimunitive David Hawk on a tear. Nato came straight for me, reaching me as the chief of police pulled up alongside.

"You stupid maniac," Nato fumed. "I suppose you have an explanation for upsetting our factory schedule like this. Who are these idiots? What do you think you're doing?"

I let him fume and rant, waiting for the chief of police to get out of his car and join us. When he did, I signaled for Nashima. She got out quickly.

"Chief Takamora," she said. "I am Nashima Porfiro, president of the Porfiro Toy Company. I accuse this man, Nato Nakuma, of being a member of the Sons of August Six. I accuse him of threatening me and my bloodline with extinction. I accuse Nato Nakuma of masterminding a plot to murder more than two million American children, plus their families, on Christmas day. I accuse . . ."

The chief held up his hand, muttering something in Japanese. Nashima blushed, bowed an apology and repeated her accusations in Japanese. In her excitement, she'd forgotten that the chief didn't understand English.

When she was finished, the chief looked at Nato Nakuma, still fuming, his cigar stoking up to a wild fury, then gazed back at the line of cars that stretched all the way to the street and beyond. He cracked something in Japanese and Nashima responded. She turned to me and whispered: "He wants to know who these people are. What should I tell him?"

I whispered back: "Tell them they're all your relatives. That'll give Nato and his black-hooded friends something to think about the next time they feel like making threats against you."

She spoke to the chief, who listened then turned to Nato Nakuma. They spoke at length. I could see Nashima's anger growing.

"What the hell are they talking about?" I asked.

"He told the chief that I am nominal president of the company, but do not have the mental aptitude of a child of six, that I was unsuitable for executive position, that I am a troublemaker, that my accusations are stupid and asinine."

"Tell the chief we have proof. Tell him what's in the warehouse."

Nashima cut in on Nato Nakuma's little tirade, speaking softly but rapidly in Japanese. The chief said something to Nato, who shrugged and gave the chief a key to the warehouse. I felt a pang of doubt then. The man was up to something.

"What's happening?" I asked Nashima in another whisper, although I had a good idea.

"Nato says the warehouse is empty. The chief can see for himself. A full shipment of robots left Hiroshima last night, he said, but production continues. The chief can inspect the factory if he wishes."

I didn't figure he would wish, once he found the warehouse empty. Nashima could demand an inspection, but it would be cursory. As for the room that I suspected held the explosives, I was certain that Nato Nakuma had been tipped off by the police chief after Nashima's call and had cleaned it out. The toy robots now being packed for shipping would be clean.

And there was all our proof, up in smoke. All except the Tikki-Tik Nashima and I had stolen from the shipping room. I'd left it back at the Christian Youth Home, convinced that I wouldn't need it as evidence.

And I wouldn't. The police chief would merely shrug it off, insist that I'd put the explosives there to incriminate an honest businessman like Nato Nakuma. And he'd get very curious about my role in this, ask questions I couldn't answer, possibly turn me over to immigration.

It was best for me to take a secondary role here.

As an exercise in futility, I followed the cops and Nakuma to the warehouse, waited for the chief to open the door and followed everyone inside.

The warehouse was indeed empty, but I knew where the contents were.

They were aboard the *Endiro Gotsu*—already on their way to the United States.

NINETEEN

Nashima had been right about the police. Either the chief was a member of the Sons of August Six or was under threat from them. The police inspection of the factory was so cursory, there was no interruption of production.

Tikki-Tiks kept rolling through the assembly line like rabbits being turned out in wholesale litter.

They weren't armed with explosives, but I knew they would be as soon as we left, or shortly after.

And the room that I was convinced held the TNT packets was opened for inspection, at Nashima's demand. It held several file cabinets of company records. Each cabinet had a nice layer of dust, as though it hadn't been moved in years.

When it was all assessed, Nashima and I felt lucky to come away without being arrested for disturbing the peace, snarling traffic, breaking and entering and damaging company property. The police chief gave Nashima a long lecture in Japanese—I didn't even bother to ask what he said. Her face told me it wasn't good.

It took the better part of an hour to sort out Nashima's relatives from the motorists who'd joined our caravan along the way. They were all having great fun and hoped we would do it again someday.

As I drove the little Honda away, heading north, Nashima turned to me. .

"We must not return to the Christian Youth Home," she said. "I have offended the Sons of August Six by telling the police of their threat. Even though the police chief is obviously one of them, that won't matter. They will carry out their threat on me and my bloodline."

"Where do you suggest we go?"

I knew, of course, where *I* had to go. Nato Nakuma had said that the toy robots were already aboard the *Endiro Gotsu* heading for San Francisco. I had to find out exactly when she sailed and track her course through the Pacific.

Once I had the data I needed, I'd contact Hawk and have him get the U.S. Navy in on the act.

But I couldn't just lob off in my own direction now. Nashima and her relatives were in extreme danger because of me, because they had made the effort to help me, help America. There was plenty of time to stop that ship, if only Hawk would listen to me. Meanwhile, I'd stay with Nashima until I could be certain she and her family—and Kiko Shoshoni—were safe.

"I have been thinking," Nashima said. "It is time for my family to stand firm. I have trusted man-servants at my home. There is a wall. With proper arms and proper discipline, we could turn it into a fortress."

"Unless the Sons have already gone in and leveled it."

"Let us go and find out."

This lady wasn't soft, far from it. She was gutsy from the word go.

By the time we'd reached Nashima Porfiro's quiet residential neighborhood, I'd convinced the relatives behind us to stop blowing their horns. They didn't even have their headlights on. We circled the block, saw that nothing seemed amiss on the grounds, then I steered the Honda up the long, winding driveway to the mansion. Toko, the big, hulking man-servant, came out to greet us.

Nashima spoke with him at length in Japanese. He waved to the others to put their cars, jeeps and trucks in the back yard. Nashima turned to me.

"Toko says the Sons came last night in their black hoods. They believed him when he pleaded ignorance to my whereabouts. But he says they have been watching the house ever since. They know we're here."

"Are he and the other servants willing to help, to fight?"

She nodded. "They are. Toko has known about the initial threat to me for a long time. He and the others have a stash of weapons in the wine cellar. We shall be well defended."

We went inside and I went directly to the wine cellar. There were fifty M-16 automatic rifles. There were boxes and boxes of hand grenades. There were bazookas and mortars, with ample ammunition. There were even thousands of Chinese firecrackers to be used to confuse the enemy, make him think he was being resisted by a formidable army.

For the next two hours, after everyone had eaten a necessary dinner, I gave lessons on the use of the M-16s, the grenades, the bazookas and mortars. No lessons were necessary on the firecrackers. While several husky nephews and cousins were helping the man-servants seal the front and rear gates with huge chains, I got Nashima aside.

"At dark, I leave," I said. "I have work to do."

"You will call the U.S. Navy, send them after the ship?"

"I've been thinking about that," I said, "among a lot of other things. First of all, just stopping that ship won't halt the flow of these booby-trapped toys into the United States or other countries that were our Allies during World War Two. I have to set up the machinery to destroy the factory."

"There must be some other way," she pleaded.

"I could easily kill Nato Nakuma," I said, "but another black-hood would take his place. If I don't find a way to destroy the factory, it will keep pumping out these robots, packing them with explosives and sending them off on other ships.

Eventually, one or two—or more—of the ships will get through. If that happens, it becomes a matter of logistics, a complicated puzzle that will spread like disease throughout the world. Thousands would die, in spite of our efforts."

"But isn't the primary thing to find and have the U.S. Navy stop the first ship?"

"Maybe. I'll get through to Hawk and see what he has to say."

"Yes?"

"But, even if he does agree to call in the Navy, that could turn into a catastrophe."

"How so?"

"I doubt if we could get any Navy captain to fire on that ship from a distance. Especially with innocent seamen aboard. And, if any warship stops that cargo vessel carrying those robots, there will certainly be a few members of the Sons of August Six aboard. They'll blow themselves up, taking the warship along with them. It's what we call being between a rock and a hard place."

There was another matter to be taken care of, another base to touch, but I didn't tell her about it. It involved Tumio, the enigmatic brother she did not want to talk about.

She sighed. "I thought I had a difficult time ahead of me," she said wistfully. "Your job will be much more difficult, more complicated and more dangerous."

I shrugged. I did that to hide the fear that was building inside me. Not fear of being killed in whatever scheme I devised.

It was fear of failing.

I had to stop *all* those booby-trapped toys, not just one shipload of them. Even if I succeeded in destroying the factory, I knew that thousands had already been shipped from the factory to loading docks.

Were other ships already afloat, heading for Australia or Europe or Canada? Or even Hawaii? I thought of that December day more than thirty-five years ago when Japanese planes had bombed Pearl Harbor in Hawaii. Was another December 7th kind of devastation on its way to Pearl Harbor?

I had to find out. And I had to stop them.

And I hadn't the slightest idea of how to go about it.

Tumio was a longshot. But, somehow, I figured he was either the key or the means to locate it.

TWENTY

The Boeing 727 cut down through thick clouds and suddenly there were the brilliant lights of Tokyo. As the plane was taxiing up the long tube that would latch onto the doorway like a leech, I tried not to remember the last time I'd flown in here.

But the memories came. They were never far away.

This time, there was no black-hooded execution squad waiting at the end of the tunnel. I swished through the airport without hindrance, waited in baggage for my small suitcase, took the monorail into the city center, then hopped a cab for the ride out to Arakawa-ku, in the northern part of the city.

"Take me to 47713 Kototai-dori, and don't pretend you don't understand my damned English. I'm in no mood for screwing around."

"Yes sir," he said, hauling ass out into traffic. "I understand good."

There had been no trouble leaving Hiroshima; that was the last thing Nato Nakuma and his terrorists expected of me. The only trouble had been in leaving Nashima.

It wasn't only that I was worried about her and her relatives defending themselves in that mansion. It was several other things, not the least of which was the chemical attraction that I felt for her.

That one swift hour of love-making in the home of the missionaries had merely whetted my appetite. I wanted that lady more than ever, and was beginning to doubt that we'd ever find the time or the place for at least one more sweet hour of absolute bliss.

Another reason was that I was pretty well convinced that I would have to take the life of at least one of Nashima's relatives, one of her bloodline.

Unless Tumio came up with just the right answers, the big .45 that I'd concealed in my one suitcase would boom once again. This time at a human target.

Quite frankly, I was angry. Angry with the black-hooded thugs, angry with fate, angry with myself. So far, I'd done little else but get myself screwed at every turn on this crazy assignment.

I was tired, to put it another way, of being beaten and disbelieved, of crying in the wrong towel, of missing my targets by inches—or by minutes.

It was time for Nick Carter, N3, Killmaster for AXE, to get back on the winner's track. Maybe Tumio held the key, maybe not. Shortly, I'd find out.

When the taxi let me out at the drugstore near

Tumio's apartment, I phoned him.

"*Ohio*," he said, gloomily.

"Michigan," I said. "Go Blue."

There was a gasp, then a long silence. I waited.

"I—uh—you—I . . ."

I waited.

Finally, he said, "What you really mean is 'go to hell, Blue.' Right?"

The coast was clear. Or he had recovered well and was lying again. But I had to take the risk.

"Right. Mix up some martinis. I'll be right up."

Actually, I didn't go right up. I circled his apartment building, went inside, walked up to his floor, cased the corridors for ten minutes, then finally knocked on his door. He opened it instantly.

"Hey, where's the broad smile?" I asked the incredibly handsome man. Now, I could see the resemblance to Nashima.

He dashed through the doorway, looked up and down the corridor, came inside and closed the door.

"My God," he said, sounding just like Nashima. "You've signed my death warrant coming here."

"Sit down," I said. "Listen up good, then I have some questions. But first, let's have those martinis."

As I talked, I moved around his apartment, peeking into closets, the bathroom, the bedroom, behind the furniture—even out the window. The place was clean, unless the black-hooded thugs had flattened themselves out under the carpet.

I sat in the comfortable Western-style chair, sipped my martini and told Tumio that I knew he was Nashima's brother, and that he had lied to me about the cost of the Tikki-Tik robots. I then told him what was going on in Hiroshima. When I told him how the clan had gathered to fight the monstrous threat from the Sons of August Six, he paled and began to stammer again.

"Don't worry," I said. "They're well armed and the black-hooded gents are very busy trying to get their other act in shape. They're speeding up production on the toy robot. One ship has already left for the States. I'm here for a variety of reasons. One is to find out just where you stand in all this, find out why you lied to me about the cost of the toy and to enlist your aid in my next plan."

He shook his head, slowly but emphatically.

"I cannot help you," he said.

"Why not?"

"Everything was going well," he said, looking at me with a plea in his eyes, "until you called me from Hiroshima. Let me explain."

"I think you'd better."

Tumio, it seemed, was not Tumio at all. His name was Hashito Anjino, named after his grandfather. When the Sons of August Six made their first threat against the family, young Hashito was out of town. His sister, Nashima, took the brunt of the threat. She told them that her brother had run away to the United States, that there was only herself, her aged father and her retarded brother left in the main family.

The story worked because Hashito had been planning a trip to the States, had obtained a passport and a visa, plus airline tickets. Nashima knew all this. Her only alteration in the story was that her brother had run away, rather than face family and company responsibilities. He was, she told the black hoods, a congenital coward.

In truth, Tumio—or Hashito—had gone to the northern island of Hokkaido to say goodbye to relatives. He was leaving for the United States to study to become a minister. Carl and Joan Jordan had made all the arrangements.

"Nashima contacted me at an uncle's house," Hashito said, "and warned me not to take the plane on which I was scheduled to leave. She told me to come to Tokyo, take an apartment under the name of Tumio Hakato and wait for further instructions. When that plane was blown up during the takeoff, I realized the seriousness of the problem. Later, when money in the family became tight, Nashima managed to get me a job with the Tokyo office of our own company, under the assumed name, of course."

He'd been living peacefully that way for a whole year. But when David Hawk called Nashima, she put him in touch with Tumio, saying only that he was a trusted vice president. Her intentions had been to use her brother only as a go-between, someone to supply weapons and simple advice. He was the only person in Tokyo she could trust.

Complicated? Not to the Oriental mind. It all made perfect sense to Nashima and Hashito.

They'd both been waiting for some future day when they could eradicate the black-hooded thugs and regain family control once again. Revenge is a long-range trait in the Oriental mind. I could easily understand the ferocity of the Sons of August Six, after more than thirty-five years.

In the minds of such men, revenge will be alive and well after thirty-five *hundred* years.

I felt a bit ticked off at Nashima for not telling me all this before, but I suppose she hadn't grown a full trust in me.

"And the day you gave me that phony figure for the selling price of the robot," I said. "Did you have a gun at your head?"

"Yes. I was caught in the advertising department when I went to look at the secret campaign plans. I told a convincing story, I thought, but three black-hooded men arrived at my apartment the night you called. They seemed to know that you'd call. They told me the figure to give and made me hang up right away."

"Do they know your real name?"

"No, thank God. That's why I was so flustered when you called. I thought I'd seen the last of you. I know they're watching my apartment. They know you're here."

"Then why did you give the signal that the coast is clear?"

He sagged in his chair, reached out to me with pleading hands.

"I am tired, Mr. Carter. Tired of hiding, tired of using a fake name, tired of being afraid. I suppose something inside me snapped then. As much as I feared your coming, I wanted an end to all this trouble and sneaking about."

"Then you no doubt understand why Nashima and the rest of your kin are now holed up in a homemade fortress."

"Yes. I understand. Living under such a threat for so long can take an enormous toll. They are ready to fight."

"What about you? Are you ready to fight? Or just give up?"

He tried one of those patented smiles, but it didn't quite come off.

"I am ready to fight," he said without much conviction. "Just tell me what you want me to do."

"I have a plan to halt the production of booby-trapped toys," I said. "Initially, I figured I'd have to destroy the factory to do it. If I destroy the factory, I destroy your family's livelihood. No insurance company would pay off if they found out the factory was using unauthorized explosives."

"What made you suspect that Nato Nakuma and his evil partners were using explosives?" Hashito asked.

"A number of things. Nakuma was too pat in his story that an American competitor planted explosives there. It was as though he wanted anti-American sentiment to be stirred up. That's a trademark of the Sons of August Six. And he was so secretive and touchy about the toy itself. I developed a theory that perhaps the explosion was accidental, occurring when someone in the shipping room dropped some explosives or made a mistake in setting a timer. The tough part was in proving my theory, but it's been proved, my friend. In spades."

"And what do you need of me?"

"You're Japanese," I said. "I need you to do some checking for me, things only a Japanese can do. I want to know which ships Nakuma is using to send his toys to the States and to other countries who were our allies in World War Two. I want exact schedules. And then, of course, there's my plan to save the factory."

"And what is your plan?"

"I'll tell you on the plane back to Hiroshima."

He paled again. "Is it necessary that I return there?"

"Not only necessary," I said. "Essential."

I gave him ten minutes to pack a small bag. I still didn't know if I could trust him, even if he were Nashima's brother. And, if I could trust him, how did I know his cowardice wouldn't override his determination to be clear of the threat?

Nashima's cover story to keep her brother from harm had been believed because it was so believable.

On the way down in the elevator to the garage where Tumio kept his car, his nervousness was catching. My old paranoia began to work. It's a good thing it did. I became wary and used caution.

"Wait," I said as I left the elevator and started down a narrow, dimly lighted corridor toward the basement garage. "Keep the elevator doors open and ready. In case we have to beat a hasty retreat, this is our only way out of this hole."

He held the elevator doors open and I crept down the corridor to a metal door. The upper part of the door was glass. I peered through, saw only cars out there in the even darker garage.

I waited, letting my eyes become accustomed to the darker area, scanning the cars and the concrete wall across the way. Nothing. Still, my spy sense of danger was rattling around. I waited another full minute and motioned for Tumio to follow.

I opened the door, gun in hand, and stepped into the garage. I let the door close behind me, motioning Tumio to hold back. I could actually *feel* human presence in that big, drafty garage.

But I couldn't see anyone.

I took two steps forward. My eyes were sweeping the cars on the left when I saw motion directly across from me. A whole volley of shots cut loose.

It was Tokyo International Airport all over again.

Three men had stepped from behind cars across the way, were backed against the wall, their automatic rifles belching flame and fury.

Three men in black hoods.

I hit the pavement and opened up with the old .45.

TWENTY–ONE

The gun boomed so loudly in the huge garage that I thought my eardrums had burst. When I fired the second round, I didn't hear the sound.

But the gun was working slickly. I could tell by the heavy jolt the slide was giving me each time I fired.

Bullets from the three rifles against the back wall shattered the glass in the door behind me, plunked sickeningly into the concrete walls. I just hoped Tumio had hit the dirt or gotten the hell out of that narrow hallway.

Bullets started to hit the wall closer to me and I made a quick roll to my right, toward a red Datsun. One of the hooded gunmen anticipated my move and blew the hell out of the car. The gastank exploded in a ball of raging flame.

I used the furious distraction to dash past the Datsun. I did a somersault along the wall and came to my knees about five cars down, directly in front of a big Lincoln. I eased between the Lincoln and a Toyota, took a bead on the man who'd just killed the Datsun and squeezed off a shot.

The gun bucked in my hand. A tongue of flame leaped from the barrel and I heard another cartridge click into place. My hearing had come back. I heard the boom almost as an echo, just as the man across the way started his slow descent to the pavement, and to death.

I was just aiming at the man on the right when both remaining men spotted my position.

Quick. No time for aiming.

I emptied the clip, letting the gun buck and jolt and sway in my hand that was rapidly growing tired.

A pain ripped up through my back and I was certain one of the rifle bullets had caught me there. No, I was just paying for that somersault. I'd apparently disturbed a kidney that had been leaving me alone for a time. In effect, I'd pissed the little devil off and he was hurting like hell in retribution.

The final blast of the old .45 was just what the doctor ordered. When the gunsmoke cleared from in front of my eyes, I saw both remaining men tumbling in a heap on top of the first one.

The last man to fall was still alive, or his death agonies were still active. His rifle made a sweep in the air, plunging hot copper and steel bullets into the concrete ceiling.

And then the garage was quiet.

I lay waiting. There could be more of them. As I waited, my hearing gradually returned full force. I heard a distant car engine start, knew it was the leader of this execution squad making his getaway.

Next came footsteps, from the door I'd just come through. I raised my head and saw Nashima's brother moving cautiously into the garage. Good, he hadn't been hit. I needed the guy more than I was willing to admit—much more than *he* knew.

"One got away," I said. "The word will be out and they'll be looking everywhere for us."

"Then we can't go to Hiroshima," he said. There was a bit of hopeful expectancy in his voice. I hated to disappoint him.

"Once again, that's the last place they'd expect us to go."

"All right," he said wistfully. "My car is just down here."

"Don't you want to see the faces of the three men who tried to kill us?"

"Why? I wouldn't know them."

"You may be surprised," I said. "Come on."

I went over and removed the three hoods. The faces of two men were clear. I'd shot them in the chest. The third man had a face full of blood and a neat hole in his forehead. Exactly where I'd aimed.

There was a gasp from Tumio. He began the stammering again.

"You know these turkeys?"

"Two of them," he said. "They work in our Tokyo office. I have seen the third man in a restaurant near our office."

"Very cozy," I said. "You never know who your friends are in this country."

"Or your enemies."

Yeah. He was right about that. "Let's go," I said. "It's a long drive to Hiroshima."

Actually, I had no intentions of taking that long drive. But, if they caught up with us soon, I wanted Tumio to think it. I had the feeling that this young man didn't stand up well under threats or torture. It was more than a feeling. He'd proved it.

There was only one way out of the garage, but I was pretty certain the black-hooded people had vacated the area for now. Their fierceness seemed greater when they were incognito and up against inferior opponents. I'd proved my "superiority" by blowing away three office workers who had decided to play dangerous games.

The fourth one, the one who'd brought them here to play this particular dangerous game, had fled as soon as the shooting stopped and his side had lost. I was sure of that.

Even so, I kept low in the car as Tumio drove onto the dark street. I peered out the back window for signs of anyone following. After Tumio had driven six miles and was on the highway to Osaka, I sat up.

"All right," I said. "I figure they had someone watching from another apartment. He's notified others who have confirmed that we've left the city by car. They'll be waiting for us far down the highway. Take the exit to Yokohama. We'll get an Air Nippon milk run flight to Matsue, rent a car and drive the final thirty miles to Hiroshima."

He smiled. His first since my return. "Very clever, you Chinese," he said. "I never would have thought of such a thing."

I started to say, maybe that's why you've been hiding out and I've been risking my balls. I decided not to. I needed to build the guy up, not tear him down.

As we drove toward the Yokohama airport, I explained what I'd want of him in Hiroshima. His smile broadened. I'd told him of all the safe, gumshoe work that needed to be done. I wouldn't tell him about the killing part until I had to.

And I would have to very soon.

TWENTY–TWO

"Bad news, Nick," Nashima said on the telephone. "Nakuma has supplemented his obvious police protection by calling in all the Sons of August Six sharpshooters to replace the young guards."

I was calling from a pay phone just north of Hiroshima. It was four in the morning. Tumio—or Hashito Anjino—was waiting in the nearby rented car.

"Any other bad news? In fact, any intel you can give me before we return to the city may save our lives."

"Yes," Nashimo said sleepily. I had wakened her from a sound sleep with my unexpected early-morning call. "Production has been increased so much that another ship will be loaded this afternoon."

"Destination?"

"The United States, of course."

"Where are you getting your information, Nashima?"

I could almost see her wonderful smile through the telephone. Her voice was certainly smiling. "I have not been the leader of Porfiro Toy Company all these years for nothing," she said. "I still have friends there, trusted friends. And they have told me something that should make it easier on your Navy's conscience if it becomes necessary to sink the *Endiro Gotsu* or any other ship carrying the booby-trapped robots."

"What is that?"

"The Sons of August Six have arranged to replace all crewmen, including the captains, with their own members. There will be no innocent seamen aboard those ships."

"That is good news," I said. "In a way. In another way, it makes the job tougher. Those hard-nosed fanatics won't take warnings. We can stop them only by killing them. Well, never mind that. You stay holed up for at least another day. If my plan works, we'll have this thing wrapped up by tonight. Right now, we're going to catch some sleep and then . . ."

"You keep saying 'we,' " she interrupted. "You have someone with you?"

Tumio had asked me during the plane-and-car ride from Tokyo not to tell his sister that he was with me, unless she asked.

"I have your brother with me. He's waiting out by the highway in the car I rented in Matsue."

Even through my words, I could hear her small gasp, almost concealed by the muffling of her hand over the mouthpiece.

"You have Tumio with you? My God, Nick, why?"

I told her of what had happened in Tokyo, of the attack in the apartment garage, of our escape through Yokohama.

"Have you told him where the family clan has gathered?" she asked, her voice low and cautious. "Have you told him that we are barricaded in the great house?"

"Yeah, why?"

She took a deep breath and let it all out. "I cannot say all that needs to be said on the telephone," Nashima sighed. "I don't know what my brother has told you, Nick, but I am certain that he didn't tell you one important thing."

"And what is that?"

"That he is under a death threat from . . ."

"He told me about how the Sons of August Six had threatened to kill him, the only male Anjino heir, about his being out of town and being told by you to hide out in Tokyo. Is there something else?"

"Yes," she said. "I will explain it all when I see you. First, you must not trust Tumio. He is too cowardly to try to harm you personally, but he will not hesitate to lead you into the hands of the enemy if he thinks by so doing he will diminish the threat or danger to himself."

"I think you'd better tell me all you know, Nashima," I said. "For the next few hours, at least, I have to put a lot of trust in your brother."

She took another deep breath, let it out loudly. "Ears may be listening."

"Let them. I hope they are. They'll be damned well warned that I'm through screwing around. From now on out, I'm going for the jugular vein of anybody who gets in my way."

She told me a long and complicated family story that is so typical in some old-style Japanese families. Although she was the first born in the Anjino family, it is the first born *son* who is the legal and "logical" heir to whatever riches his father acquires. But Hashito (Tumio) had shown early on that he was cowardly, that he didn't have what it really took to handle his father's legacy. Oji Hashito Anjino had held on as long as he could and then gave the family business to Nashima and her husband, Nadita Porfiro.

"I have no proof," Nashima said, "but some members of our family are convinced that Hashito was responsible for the threat made by the Sons of August Six. Some of my uncles and cousins believe that Hashito was responsible for my husband's death. He was conveniently out of town when Nadita died, and he was conveniently out of town when the threat was made on me and my family."

"But, if he was in cahoots with the Sons of August Six," I interjected, "why did he have to stay away, hide under another name?"

"It was not fear of the Sons of August Six that he stayed away," she said. "It was fear of being killed by a family member."

"But you helped him. Why?"

There was a pause. "Even though I know there might be substance in what some members of my family believe, I cannot turn my back on my brother. And now I cannot turn my back on you. I do not wish you to harm my brother, Nick, but I also do not wish him to harm you. I merely tell you this so that you will be on guard. Watch that Hashito does not head you into the den of the Sons of August Six."

I didn't say it, but he'd already started down that road. As we'd driven down from Matsue in the rented car, he'd suggested a place where we could hide until I finalized my plans. That place, I was now certain, was where I would be betrayed, caught off guard. Once Hashito had me out of the way, he'd skip back to Tokyo and take up his life as Tumio once more.

But he knew I'd stopped here to call Nashima. Perhaps he was convinced that Nashima wouldn't warn me against him. Well, I'd just have to keep him guessing on that score.

After assuring Nashima that I'd be just fine, and warning her again to stay barricaded in the mansion until it was all over, I went out to the car. Hashito was slouched in the seat, asleep, or pretending to be asleep.

I'd started the car and was well down the highway, heading into Hiroshima, when Hashito sat up, rubbed his eyes and asked:

"Are they safe—Nashima and the rest of our family?"

I deliberately flashed him a warm, unsuspecting smile. "Snug as ships in harbor," I said.

"Did you tell Nashima that I was with you?"

"Sure. Any reason why I shouldn't have?"

He shrugged. There was a nervousness in that shrug. "No reason. Did she have anything new to report on the factory or on the activities of the Sons of August Six?"

I told him about the step-up in production, about the second ship that would be loaded late today or early tomorrow. He seemed relieved when we got off the subject of Nashima.

"Very well," he said, feeling confident and safe again. "While you are resting at the place I will take you, I will get the weapons you requested. And then we will discuss your plan and put it into action."

I hadn't told him my plan because, frankly, I really didn't have one solidified in my mind. We couldn't go to the police, I couldn't call Hawk for backup, another raid on the factory would turn out just as silly and ridiculous as the last one. And, even if I did have a specific plan, I wouldn't dare tell Hashito about it. Not now, not after what Nashima had told me.

And I couldn't let him lead me to that "safe" place he'd talked about.

But I had a sudden brainstorm. There was one place I could go and be safe. Meanwhile, I'd have to string along with Hashito.

I followed his directions and we soon were in an old residential area just off the business section. I parked the rented car a block away from an old house he indicated. We walked in the early morning darkness to the house, entered through a back door that had a faulty lock and Hashito led me to a bedroom on the second floor.

"You will be safe here," he said, looking around, his old nervousness back. "This house once was occupied by my father's mistress. After he became incapacitated, he sent his mistress away, but has kept the house ready for the time he is well enough to bring her back. Except that he will never be well. He is too old and the stroke was too devastating."

"Very convenient," I said. "Where will you get the Luger and the stiletto."

I didn't trust the .45 or the hunting knife I'd been using as my main weapons. Hashito had assured me that, through contacts, he could obtain any weapons I wished. It was important, he said, that he go alone for them. He'd be going into a section of Hiroshima where Westerners were unwanted. The few who strayed there never came out alive.

His story was believable and, to cap it off, here was the house he'd told me about. I would be safe here until he returned with a Luger and a stiletto. As for gas bombs, he'd never heard of such devices, so I'd have to make my attack without that trusty and highly effective weapon.

I would have gone along completely with his plan, but for the warning from Nashima.

And, within the hour, I would have been dead.

As soon as Hashito left, I went downstairs and found the telephone on a table in the living room. I memorized the number and then slipped out the back door. Hashito had taken the rented car, so I hoofed it out to Kiko Shoshoni's apartment.

The apartment seemed cold and lonely without Kiko, but I was glad she was safe with Nashima and the others at the Porfiro mansion. Sleepy as I was, I sat by the telephone, watching the dawn come.

Precisely two hours after Hashito had left me, I called the number I'd memorized. It rang several times and I was about to hang up when someone picked up the receiver. I could hear that someone breathing.

"Hashito Anjino," I said.

The breathing stopped, then there was a gasp. I heard clunking sounds as the phone was being put down. I waited.

"*Ohio,*" Hashito's voice said, cautiously, tentatively.

"Michigan," I said. "Go Blue."

"Mr. Carter," he said between gasps. "Where are you? I was so worried when I returned and found you gone. Have they—has someone kidnapped you?"

I didn't want to play any more games with this punk.

"Who answered the phone?"

"I—I did. I was afraid of who it would be. That's why I let it ring so many times, why I was reluctant to speak. When I returned and found the house empty, I was terrified that they'd taken you and were calling to learn if I had returned."

"Yeah," I said, not believing a word he was

saying. "I'll bet you were terrified. Look, Hashi-to, I have a few things to tell you."

I told him everything that Nashima had revealed to me. He gasped a number of times. He tried to interrupt, to deny. I barreled on, ignoring his protests. When I was finally finished, I could hear him breathing hard into the mouthpiece. I could also hear someone else breathing.

"Nashima does not have all the truth," he said. "There are many things involved here. Let me tell—"

"Don't tell me anything," I cut him off. "Show me. Do you have the weapons I asked for?"

"I do. If you'll tell me where you are, I'll be most happy—"

"I'm sure you will. You'll also be most happy to deliver the weapons to a place I designate. Right?"

"Of course."

I gave him directions. He balked, several times, but I insisted. He finally agreed.

Twenty minutes later, I left the taxi at the edge of the park and walked quickly toward the big ruined building, situated at the opposite end of the park from the Peace Memorial and bell tower.

It was still dark inside, although the sun had crested the horizon and was streaking between the tall buildings of the downtown section. I settled on the third floor.

I had no gas bombs, but I still had the three hand grenades I'd borrowed from the stash of weapons kept by Nashima's servants. I laid the grenades out on the littered floor, side by side. I put the extra clips for the .45 in a row beside the grenades. I was ready.

Five minutes later, two huge black limousines circled the park. I saw sun glinting off twin circles of glass behind one of the windows of the trailing limo. Binoculars. They were watching the old building for signs of me.

I eased back, out of view. When I peeked again, the limousines were stopped on the grass of the curb lawn between the sidewalk and the street. Four men got out of each limousine. They walked cautiously across the wet grass, watching the old building, but heading for a small pond nearer the center of the park.

I'd told Hashito Anjino to wrap the Luger and the stiletto in paper and to drop the package in a trash container at the northern end of the park.

Just as the eight men from the two limos began to veer off toward the old building, obviously to set up a gun station to kill me when I turned up to claim the weapons, I saw the rented car circle the park and stop fifty yards ahead of the limos.

Hashito got out, carrying something under his arm. Something wrapped in newspapers. He made a beeline for the pond and the trash container.

I heard footsteps below, knew that the men were coming up. But not all of them—there were not enough footsteps. I leaned out through a jagged hole and saw five of them patrolling below.

The footsteps came closer and I felt nervous.

Sweat covered my forehead with a slick sheen and collected in my palms. But I watched the men below, waiting for them to get into a position more favorable to my plans.

The footsteps of the three men reached the second floor. I had only a few seconds to take care of the outside threat. The men were separated into two groups—three to the right of me, two to the left.

Quietly, I pulled the pins on two grenades, held the levers in place, waiting for the last moment. The men didn't join up. I'd have to be damned accurate with those grenades.

I tossed the first one at the group of three, then shifted the second one to my right hand and tossed it at the group of two. I'd let go of the timing levers at different intervals. Both grenades had to go off simultaneously—in four seconds.

The footsteps reached the third floor landing.

Below, the grenades went off, one a split-second behind the other.

Screams rent the dawn air and, with the twin explosions, shredded the peace and calm of the park.

The footsteps out on the landing thundered on the steps as the three men who'd been coming up to find a vantage point to kill me when I came to pick up the weapons stormed back outside. I saw Hashito stop on the grass, the package still gripped under his arm. He was gaping at the place where the two grenades had knocked off five of his Sons of August Six friends.

And then he saw me. His mouth dropped open

and he pointed up at me. I leaned out, saw the three remaining Sons scamper down the stairs. They hadn't seen Hashito. I aimed the .45.

Hashito screamed at his friends. They looked up and started drawing weapons.

I lobbed a grenade at them and aimed the .45 at Hashito. Nashima had said she didn't want him harmed. But there was no way around this treacherous bastard.

I squeezed the trigger. The old .45 boomed and bucked in my hand. A hot whizzer of lead burst from the barrel as the slide jerked back and forth, ejecting the spent shell and clicking a new cartridge into lethal position.

Even from the great distance, I could see the neat round hole in Hashito's forehead. He just stood there, for what seemed an eternity. And then he fell forward, like a stiff pine tree, and crashed facedown in the soft, wet grass.

Even before his body hit the ground, the third grenade blew like the hounds of hell just below me. I looked down, saw that the three men had spread out, that the grenade had blown only one of them to bits.

The other two were crouched, making smaller targets, weapons aimed up at the jagged hole on the building's third floor.

I let them blast away for a full minute. Chunks of stone and wood and plaster flew back through the room. There was a pause and I knew both men were reloading at the same time.

I moved into the hole, took aim on the man on

the right, and heard the distant police sirens. A bunch of them.

I lost no time dispatching the two remaining Sons. The first took a hot pellet in his chest. From the high angle of fire, the bullet must have traveled through his heart, liver, stomach and at least one of his kidneys. He died in place, falling over on his side without coming out of his crouch.

The second man managed to leap to his feet, trying desperately to slip a cartridge into the cylinder of a .38 revolver. My ounce-plus of fiery lead caught him in the throat. He dropped his pistol, clutched his throat, but could not stem the gushing tide of blood that squirted between his fingers.

I could hear him gagging and coughing all the way up to the third floor.

In the name of mercy, I let fly another death pellet. It struck him between the eyes and he slumped instantly to the ground, dead. No longer gagging and coughing. No longer in pain.

And no longer a threat.

I quickly gathered up my remaining clips and fled the building. The sirens were getting louder.

I set out across the lawn toward the rented car Hashito had driven to this place of ambush. As I passed his still body, I snatched up the bundle he had dropped and opened it.

Nothing.

The sirens screamed louder and, in the distance, I could see a whole caravan of police cars, lights going crazy, wheels spinning and squealing through the thickening traffic.

I trotted easily to the rented car and found luck going my way for a change.

Not only were the keys in the ignition, but the police cars screaming to find out who'd shattered the silence of Peace Park were being held up by a knot of traffic at a distant intersection.

I started the car and drove slowly away.

But I'd won only one small round in a long and bloody fight.

Without a definite plan, without adequate help—and with one ship already on its way to the United States with its dangerous cargo—the outcome of all future rounds was not really in much doubt.

There was doubt, for instance, that I was involved in a fight that I couldn't possibly win.

Somehow, that knowledge took all the fun out of having just won a round with the Sons of August Six.

TWENTY–THREE

A kind of exhaustion had set in by the time I got back to Kiko's empty apartment. I felt safe enough to catch a few winks of sleep, but I didn't want to waste the time.

One shipload of the lethal robots was already at sea, probably around the southern tip of Japan by now and heading out into the Pacific. And, within hours, a second ship would be loaded and ready to follow. Yet lack of sleep and a growing ache in my sore kidneys were affecting my ability to think, to plan.

There had to be a way to stop Nato Nakuma . . . there had to be a way to stop the *Endiro Gotsu* without getting an American shipful of innocent sailors blown to bits.

It was the ship, more than the lack of a plan on how to stop more booby-trapped robots from leaving the country, that finally caused me to try to contact Hawk. After all, once I explained the ticklish situation to him, surely he'd be able to get the Navy to intercept the *Endiro Gotsu* and send it back to Japan. Or to blow it out of the water from a distance.

I made the call to Washington collect, uncaring whether Hawk would object, or even whether the phone was being tapped.

"This is N3," I told the agent who responded. I put through my code and requested to speak with the chief.

"Sorry, N3. He isn't here."

"Then, put me through to his home."

"No good," the agent said. "He's out with the commander-in-chief. Not to be disturbed."

I gave the agent a message for Hawk. All about the ship loaded with booby-trapped robot toys, about other ships to come. He cut me short.

"Sorry, N3. Our instructions are clear and simple. You're to work it out all by yourself."

He clicked off. I held a dead phone in my hand. I listened to see if some interloper had tapped in. Nothing.

I was so tired, so sleepy, so achy.

I fished in Kiko Shoshoni's bathroom medicine chest, looking for aspirin, but found none. I lay back on her bed and reviewed my position.

My only allies—Nashima and her relatives—were holed up in a walled mansion surrounded by the enemy. Even if I could enlist their aid on another raid of the factory, Nato Nakuma would be tipped off, would have his backside covered and show an empty warehouse and empty munitions room.

But the last time, I knew, Nato Nakuma hadn't

been tipped off by Nashima or her relatives. The tipoff had come when Nashima had called the police to get them there for the finale after we crashed the gates and took over. Someone from the police—perhaps the chief himself—had tipped Nakuma that we were coming, giving him time to hide all the evidence.

Next, there'd be no help from Stateside. As Hawk had said from the beginning, I was on my own, without portfolio. It would do no good even to go to the local embassy or consulate. They'd only check with the president and he'd tell them what Hawk had already told me he'd tell them.

We don't know anyone by the name of Nick Carter. There is no such American agent in Japan, or anywhere for that matter.

And I couldn't contact the local U.S. Naval attaché, even to give a friendly warning.

The police, obviously, were out.

As for weapons, I needed far more than a Luger and a stiletto, more than the .45 and the hunting knife. More, even, than the grenades and bazookas that Nashima's servants had assembled at the mansion.

I needed my own air force, my own supply of bombs.

Since the *Endiro Gotsu* had been gone two days, traveling at probably thirty knots, it was at least two hundred miles out to sea by now. More by the time I got it all together and went after her.

All right. I needed a flying machine that would haul me and a load of bombs over a distance of more than four hundred miles.

But where was I to get the bombs?

I sat up in Kiko's bed, the hair on the back of my neck sticking out like the ruff on an angry dog's.

The answer was simple. So simple that I almost blushed for not having thought of it before.

I could get the bombs I needed. It would be dangerous, and the odds were so far against me that I didn't like to think of them, but it *might* work.

Forty minutes later, I eased the rented car into the gravel parking area beside Kai Tai's Flying Service. Kai Tai was alone in the hangar, his head shoved through the open cowling of a helicopter engine. He was covered with grease, all four-feet-eleven of him.

"*Ohio,* Kai Tai," I said, grinning in anticipation of his anger.

He spun around, recognizing me instantly. He held a massive wrench in his small hand.

"You, miserable Yankee slime," he snarled. "See engine? Big great hole in cylinder block. Where you fly this machine?"

I understood his anger. And I understood the shining wrench that glinted in his hand.

"I'll pay for that, Kai Tai. I would have done it right off if I hadn't had an important appointment to keep. I . . ."

"Pay now. Six hundred dollar. U.S. Not yen."

I paid him the six hundred, though I knew it was a ripoff. No bullet had hit that engine or I wouldn't have made it back the day I'd rented the little chopper. But I was in no position to quibble.

He took the money, counted it carefully, put it into his grimy overalls pocket and eyed me suspiciously. "Wat want now?"

"I want another machine," I said, "but you have my personal guarantee that it will be returned without a scratch on it."

"No want personal guarantee. Want personal money. Fee double from last time. Also want thousand dollar deposit fee."

That came to twelve hundred dollars. I had thirteen. I gave him the whole wad, knowing I'd need nothing for the bombs, except perhaps a large portion of my own body—perhaps even my life.

He counted the money, stuck it into his pocket with the six hundred, then eyed me just as suspiciously as before.

"Why the extra hundred clams?"

"I want a little renovation job on the machine you rent me," I said. I explained what I wanted.

"All that on one miserable hundred dollar?" he exploded.

"You won't do it?"

"Kai Tai not fool. Where you plan to take machine. Two tanks give five hundred miles. You fly Tokyo, sell machine on black market?"

"I'll be using it locally," I lied. "I have a lot of ground to cover in this part of Japan."

"Liar," he snarled. "No deal, Yankee. You go now. Kai Tai got work to do fixing cylinder from last covering of wargrounds."

He was rapidly pissing me off.

"All right," I said, running a small test on Kai Tai. "If you won't do what I ask, give me my thirteen hundred dollars back."

He turned and grinned at me. "Wat thirteen hundred dollar?"

Okay, so he planned to keep the money, figuring I'd call the police who would naturally side with a respectable Hiroshima businessman. He'd flunked the test and there was only one thing I could do. I glanced around the hangar to make certain we were alone, then took out the .45. I reached out and put the cold barrel squarely between his eyes.

"Pick out your best machine," I snarled, "put two extra tanks on the thing and prepare it for a long flight. One word of argument, and all your brains will wind up on that engine behind you."

It took him an hour, in spite of his cursing, mumbling and casting murderous looks at me. He was an expert mechanic and he did a superb job. After all, it would do him no good to sabotage one of his own machines. He wasn't insured and his business was so marginal that, even with his casual thievery, he was barely making ends meet.

"You keep the money," I said as I climbed into the cockpit. "It's more than enough to pay for all your labors. If I can, I'll get this back to you in one piece."

"You better, Yankee. I give three hours, then call police."

I smiled at him and kicked over the engine. The blades began to swirl and Kai Tai backed up to save his head from being lopped off.

"See you in three hours," I shouted above the screeching whine of the engine.

I yanked back on the collective pitch stick and the little two-seater Bell rose like magic into the clear blue sky. I moved the cyclic pitch stick forward and zoomed off westward.

I knew the air route well by now. Out over the river, I moved the cyclic pitch stick to the left and turned south.

Heading for the bombs I needed to stop that ship.

Or heading to my death.

TWENTY–FOUR

The chopper hummed and throbbed like a happy insect at the height of the mating season. I stayed to the opposite side of the Ota River, high above farmland, to keep a low profile.

It wouldn't do to set tongues buzzing down there in the city or to have one of the police helicopters come up to check me out. My weapons were slim and low.

There were no grenades left from the bunch given me by one of Nashima's servants. I had only one spare clip for the old .45. The gun itself had only three cartridges left in it.

Even from the great distance, I could see the Porfiro mansion on a middle island. It was on a knoll of rolling lawns and lovely trees. I had a strong urge to see Nashima's lovely face just one more time before I went on this stupid kamikaze mission. And somebody ought to know what I was planning, just in case I failed—a highly likely prospect.

I laid the cyclic pitch stick far to the left and the

Bell dipped that way. I eased forward on the collective pitch control and began a slow, floating descent toward a wide patch of lawn behind the mansion.

My eyes alternated between checking out the place I'd chosen to set the chopper down and checking the streets around the walls of the mansion.

The Sons of August Six were there—I saw them in cars and even out strolling along the outer part of the wall. At a quick count, I could see that less than twenty were on guard at this early morning hour. It would do no good to try to kill the bastards, I reasoned. Within minutes, the various chiefs of the secret organization would have replacements, probably even doubling the guard.

As the chopper came to rest and I cut the engine, I saw the glint of sunlight off steel at every rear window of Nashima's house. Guns. They didn't know who the hell I was and they were taking no chances.

I slid back the bubbletop and hopped out quickly, waving my arms. I heard a bolt being slapped down, indicating that a lethal cartridge was in place and a nervous finger was on the trigger.

"It's me," I shouted. "The American. Where is Nashima?"

Both Nashima and Kiko came dashing out the back door. Kiko ran excitedly, like a teenager. Nashima came with long, graceful strides, like the lady she was. But I could see the happy enthusiasm on her face and the sight warmed me. It almost took the onus off my worry of what lay ahead of me.

Just thinking of my plan gave me a true impression of what the young kamikaze pilots of World War Two must have felt and thought before taking off in their planeloads of explosives. For a few sweet moments there on that soft, verdant lawn, I stopped thinking of my plan.

"Oh Nick-Nick," Kiko squealed, "we thought you were dead."

I threw a puzzled look at Nashima who was just coming up behind the excited, bubbling Kiko.

"It's true," she said. "We got a call from Hashito almost two hours ago, about dawn. He said the Sons of August Six had trapped you at Peace Park and had killed you. We were about to open the gates, to give up."

"He was counting his plans before they worked out the way he'd planned them," I said.

"I beg your pardon? I don't understand."

"Let's go inside," I said. "I could use a strong cup of coffee and a couple of grenades before I go off on a little plan of my own."

At the table in the gigantic dining room, with armed relatives all around, I told of how Hashito had tried to betray me, how I had foiled the plan and killed all eight of the Sons Hashito had sent after me. Reluctantly, I told of how I'd also murdered Hashito.

To my utter shock and surprise, everyone in the room began to cheer, to applaud. Nashima explained.

"Although I am saddened by the death of my own blood brother, I cannot say that I am truly sorry. None of my relatives approved of my plan to protect Hashito. He was weak, he was cowardly, and they knew of his real alliance with the Sons of August Six. He has brought much dishonor on this house."

"My only regret," one of the cousins piped up, "is that he died instantly. I had hoped you would make him suffer a little. Even a minute would have been satisfactory."

And so it had turned out that Hashito had good reason to hide out under the name of Tumio. And yet, we had trusted him, Hawk and I. We had literally put my life in his hands. And Nashima, because of her relation to Hashito, and her shame at the dishonor he'd brought to their house, had held back the truth from me.

That holding back had very nearly led to my death.

I told the relatives about the guard contingent outside the walls, even gave them the locations of the cars and the guards on foot. Later, they decided, they'd play a little jungle warfare, sneak over the wall and cut a few throats.

I didn't want to tell the whole group what I was planning, that by nightfall there might not be any need for their help, so I pretended I had nothing further to say. Toko, the big smiling man-servant, brought me two grenades. As I was leaving, I got Nashima aside and told her my plan.

She gasped and turned pale at the end of every

sentence. Finally, unable to contain herself, she blurted: "But you cannot do this. It will mean certain death. Even if you gain the means to blow up that ship, the explosion will tear you and that little machine from the sky. Nick, please. Wait until you can reach David Hawk. Let the authorities handle the situation. There is time."

"No," I said. "Other ships are being prepared and loaded. I don't have the time to find out just which ships. If even one of them gets through, it will mean holocaust in thousands of American households on Christmas morning. If I do what I must do at the factory and then turn back the *Endiro Gotsu,* the bloodshed and the threat will be ended. The authorities will have to put a stop to the plan or risk open warfare."

"You said you would turn back the *Endiro Gotsu.* How will you do that?"

"I'll give the captain fair warning," I said. "There's a bullhorn in the chopper. If he refuses to turn back, then I'll use the other means I hope to have at my disposal."

She shook her head and gazed at me with those wide, luminous, almond eyes.

"You will surely be killed. You are a fool to do such a thing."

I grinned. "I've never pretended to be anything but a fool, Nashima. In my whole lifetime, I've learned that there are two kinds of fools. Those who screw things up and those who try to make things right again. If we didn't have so many of the first type of fools, we wouldn't have any need of my kind. But . . ." I shrugged.

She moved close and I saw two pearllike tears collecting at the corners of her eyes. She stood on tiptoe and kissed me gently on the lips.

"Go with God," she said. "I shall wait here for you."

I knew she would have insisted on coming along, but she knew my plan.

All the extra space in that little chopper would be taken up with the special bombs I hoped to acquire soon.

If I didn't, if the first part of my plan went foul, well, it was best that I be alone.

"And I shall come back here to fetch you," I said.

I crawled into the chopper, slid the bubble forward, started the engine and took off on the first segment of my kamikaze run.

TWENTY–FIVE

The hum of the engine and the throbbing of the rotor blades very nearly put me to sleep as I streaked down along the opposite riverbank, heading for a point far south of the city. The exhaustion and lack of sleep were catching up fast.

I had to pinch the tender part of my inner thigh several times to keep me alert.

When I saw the initial target far to my left, my senses went on automatic alert. I shook off the drowsiness that had been flooding through my body and turned the throttle grip harder. Airspeed eased up to a hundred and ten.

It was important that the factory guards not even know of my existence until the very last moment. I couldn't give them time to think, time to figure out my ploy. I cruised past the tiny, seemingly uninhabited islands in the Ota River, south of Hiroshima, then made a wide circle to the left and headed back north, directly over the islands.

They weren't as uninhabited as they looked. On those barren, treeless rocks in the slow-rolling river were dirt-poor peasants living in clay-and-stick hovels. I could see them gazing up at the whirlybird in wonderment and envy. I knew there were tongues buzzing down there, but at least they had no telephones to call the police about the strange bird that was now flying so low over their heads.

My plan was to come in low and make all the noise the little Bell engine would make. I feathered the chopper blades for slow descent and maximum racket.

Three hundred yards from the factory's southern fence, I slid back the bubble, felt the cool morning wind on my face. I could see the guards in the compound of the factory. They were watching the oncoming chopper. Some of them had automatic rifles raised in anticipation of my arrival.

There was a huge factory just south of the Porfiro Toy Company's grounds. I'd already checked it out and it was clean; it made carburetors for Toyotas. I hovered above this factory, my eyes on the Porfiro grounds just ahead.

All the guards rushed toward the south fence, their automatic rifles raised in anticipation of an attack. A few of them even fired at me. I could see the tongues of flame from the muzzles of the M-16s. Their aim was bad. I never heard the whine of a bullet pass the chopper. Or the sound of the engine and the feathered blades had drowned out the sound of bullets.

When all the guards were in place, I unfeathered the blades and jerked back suddenly on the collective pitch stick. The copter shot skyward in a piercing scream. I rammed forward on the cyclic and, as I approached the south fence, I pulled the pins on both my grenades and lobbed them over the side.

I didn't wait to see the explosions below. If my timing had been right, both grenades would have gone off in the midst of those guards, the sharpshooters for the Sons of August Six.

By the time I heard the muffled explosions, I was far to the west, flying only ten feet above the surface of the Ota River. Barges and sampans clogged the channel, and a huge freighter stood at the main docks far to the north. I guessed it was the second ship, waiting for its cargo of booby-trapped robots.

It didn't matter. If my plan worked, that ship would never leave port. If it didn't work, several ships just like it would soon be heading for America and other countries that had allied themselves with America against the Japanese military might of the 1940s.

Just north of the factory grounds, I made a right turn and headed inland. There were wharfs, but no large boats. I topped the small pleasure boats with only inches to spare. My diversionary attack at the south gate would leave the guards stunned for only a short time. I had to move quickly—and as silently as possible.

My target was the warehouse, north and west of the main factory. From the south fence, it was impossible for the guards to see over the three-story factory building and spot the tiny chopper as it eased up for a drop to the warehouse roof.

I had the throttle at minimum, just enough power to keep me airborne and to get me over the fence and to the warehouse roof. Ten feet above the roof, I cut the engine altogether and let the whirling blades lower me gently. The skids still hit with a sickening crunch and I waited to see if the roof would collapse under such a jolt and the weight of the chopper.

The roof held. I was out of the cockpit before the blades stopped whirling. I ducked my head and ran to the edge of the roof nearest the factory. I skimmed over a low ledge, hung for an instant by my fingertips and then dropped to the lawn below.

Adrenaline erased my exhaustion as I ran the few yards from the warehouse to the door of the shipping room office, the door Nashima and I had used the night we'd come snooping. I lurched through the door, .45 in hand.

Workers looked up in surprise, then in anger. I waved the gun at them, motioning them farther back into the factory. They started to complain, some of them even howling. I started toward the reinforced door where I knew the explosives were kept and wasn't surprised when I heard a sharp voice of command, then heavy footfalls.

Nato Nakuma was coming, as I'd hoped he would.

"So, Mr. Toy Salesman," he said, sneering and

smiling triumphantly at the same time. "Your foolishness brings you back."

He turned to a worker and started saying something in Japanese. I knew he would send the worker to fetch the guards, so I moved fast. I put a quick stranglehold on his neck and rammed the automatic pistol into the soft part of his back, against a kidney.

"I want only one thing from you," I said, keeping my hold and cutting off his breath. "The keys to the munitions room."

I relaxed my hold to let him breathe, thus talk. He started up again in Japanese and I cut off his breath again. He tried to toss me over his shoulder, using some obscure jujitsu move, so I jammed the .45 into his kidney so hard that he could only gasp and go half limp.

"The keys," I said. "In fact, I'll duck-walk you over there and you can open the damned door yourself. Let's go."

I pushed him to the door, but he made no move to get his keys. I moved my lips close to his ear.

"This has been a bad day for me," I hissed. "I've killed Hashito Anjino and upward of a dozen or more of your Sons of August Six. What I need now, to stop you and the others, is about fifty packets of those TNT loads you've been putting inside the robot toys. Either you open the door, or I kill you and take the keys and open it myself. How about it, Nato?"

He nodded. When I released him, though, and

he was fishing for his keys, he had to get in another verbal shot.

"You won't make it out of the factory compound. My guards at the south fence have spread out all around."

"Let me worry about that. I'll need a couple of your workers to haul the TNT packets out for me."

"Ask them," he said, swinging open the heavy, reinforced door. "None of them speaks English. Ask and see how far you get."

"I'll get far," I said, "because you'll be one of the workers helping me. Call one of them now. And keep it clean, Nato. As I said, this has been a bad day and it's only getting started."

He kept grinning as he and a worker gathered up two boxes of the TNT packets and started toward the door. He knew his guards, all sharpshooters, would kill me the moment I emerged.

"Not that door," I said. "Back this way."

"It won't matter which door," he said. "The guards are everywhere out there."

"We'll see."

For insurance, I picked up a small box of explosives and went after them, the box nestled under my left arm, leaving my right hand free to cover them and the gawking workers with the .45.

I punched the button to work the electric motor on the overhead door at the end of the loading dock. Beyond the open door, only fifty yards away, was the warehouse door. I leaned forward, looked left and then right.

No guards in the area, but I saw two of them far

to the right, peering nervously through the chain-link fence.

"All right. Let's go to the warehouse. You first."

Nato Nakuma was still grinning as he led the way with the heavy box of explosive packets. The worker, looking worried but still angry, followed. I punched the button to lower the garage door and leaped down to the ground as it clanged shut. I waited until Nato Nakuma and his chosen worker were at the warehouse door before sprinting yards after them.

I opened the warehouse door and the two men entered. Once again, the warehouse was filling up with crates of robots. These birds had really been working overtime. But the warehouse was empty of workers and guards now. I pointed the .45 to a section of crates piled almost to the ceiling, near a skylight.

"Up there," I said. "Take the explosives up there."

"We can't carry these heavy boxes up there," Nato complained. "Even if we do, what will it gain you? You'll be trapped on the roof."

"Let me worry about that."

He grinned. He knew.

"How did you do it?" he asked. "How did you land on the roof without us hearing you? The guards said you'd flown away to the west, across the river."

"Magic," I said. "Now, send your worker up alone and hand the boxes up to him. Tell him to smash out the skylight and push the boxes onto the roof. Tell him straight, Mr. Factory Manager, or this boom-boom stick will scatter your brains all over this warehouse."

He must have told him straight, because the worker did exactly what I'd demanded. When both men were on top of the crates, I handed up my smaller box of explosives to Nato and climbed up beside them.

"Put this out on the roof with the others," I said, giving the smaller box to Nakuma. He gave it to the worker who slid it onto the roof. "And now," I said, motioning with the gun. "Both of you get down. Stay in the warehouse where I can see you."

Nato Nakuma did a foolish thing then. Standing there on top of the crates, in a precarious position for fighting, he lashed out with his foot, hoping to kick the gun from my hand.

With an almost instinctive motion, I eluded the foot. But my finger had its own instincts. I pulled the trigger and felt the jolt of the big .45. Damn, it was dangerous to be shooting in here. A stray bullet . . .

But the bullet didn't stray. It caught Nato Nakuma in the forehead, just below his receding hairline, and blew out the entire back of his skull.

I turned to the worker and he went to his knees, thinking I would do the same to him. I merely motioned him down. He understood the universal gesture, scampered down quickly, avoiding the sticky mess that had come from Nato Nakuma's skull. He stood in the center of the warehouse, his knees knocking. Still, he glared at me with hatred. Fortunately, his fear was the greater emotion, so he did nothing foolish.

However, as I was reaching up to pull myself through the shattered skylight to the roof, the warehouse door burst open and three guards rushed in, automatic rifles at the ready. These, indeed, were different guards. There were no callow, youthlike features, no fear. Their faces were grim, hard, their eyes glinting with angry purpose.

I turned and crouched on the crates, knowing that a firefight here would send us all up in an explosive ball of fire of near-nuclear proportions. For a few heart-stopping, breathless moments, it was a grim standoff.

Finally, the worker said something in Japanese to the guards. The guards listened, but did not lower their weapons. I could shoot at them with impunity. But, if they shot at me, if they hit one of the crates or even one of the boxes we'd pushed out onto the roof, it was over for all of us.

Slowly, the guards backed out of the warehouse. I took a breath of air for the first time in what seemed to be twenty minutes.

"Thank you," I said to the worker. "Thank you for having more sense than all of us."

I skimmed through the hole in the skylight. Working quickly, but with kidneys complaining with aches and searing pains, I put the two large and one small box of explosives into the copilot's seat in the chopper. I estimated that I had nearly two hundred pounds of explosive packets altogether.

Those two hundred pounds, along with the many tons already aboard the *Endiro Gotsu,* should do the job nicely.

But that job, I knew, was still a long way off. I had to get away from the factory grounds, and the guards now knew that my helicopter was on top of the warehouse. At least three of them did, and they were no doubt spreading the word to the others, gathering them in force to cover my takeoff.

All right, I'd have to do this one perfectly. And quickly.

The shortest way out was to my immediate right, directly over the fence behind the warehouse. As I climbed in and got ready to start the engine, I could hear voices below, shouting in Japanese. They were close, very close.

The guards had also figured my best way out was to skip directly from the warehouse roof to the nearest fence. That would be toward the west, toward the river.

The guards were massing in that area, automatic rifles ready to blow me out of the sky.

This time, I didn't have to be concerned about a stray bullet hitting a cylinder block. One hot pellet of copper and steel through the floor of the chopper and into those boxes of explosives would spread me and the chopper over all six of the city's islands.

Naturally, I did the unexpected.

I worked the collective and cyclic controls furiously, the throttle full out, the blades feathered for maximum antigravity thrust. Above the roar of the engine, I could almost hear in my mind's ear all those automatic rifles down below being cocked and armed.

The chopper rose only a few feet, then veered so sharply to the left that I damned near hit the roof of the factory building with one of the skids. I didn't look back, but I could hear the chatter of automatic weapons fire from behind me. And curses. Japanese curses.

I felt something clunk into the rear of the machine, somewhere near the tail stabilizing rotor. I waited to see if the chopper would falter, wondering what Kai Tai would say if he could see me now.

Nothing faltered. The bullet had merely hit the chopper's skin and gone on through, leaving the stabilizing rotor and all other vital controls undamaged.

I set a course for one eighty, heading directly south to pick up the route the *Endiro Gotsu* might have taken on its course from Hiroshima, down the Sea of Japan, into the western Pacific.

The easy part was over.

Now, with luck, I'd launch myself, this fragile machine and almost two hundred pounds of explosives into the real battle.

But luck didn't seem to be riding with me anymore. As I sailed over the southern farmlands of Japan, I saw something white trailing down behind the helicopter.

It was aviation fuel.

That bullet hadn't hit the tail assembly—it had ruptured one of the spare tanks Kai Tai had so reluctantly installed.

TWENTY–SIX

About the time I cleared the southern coast of Japan and saw ships moving about at snails' paces below, the stream of gasoline from the ruptured spare tank had stopped. Either the tank was empty, or the bullet had hit high.

Whatever the case, I had little fuel reserves now.

I eased back on the throttle and feathered the rotors for fuel-efficient cruise speed. I picked up three ships heading east and calculated that I must be on the main shipping lane from Japan to the West Coast of the United States.

My calculations appeared to be accurate. I was on a heading of seventy-eight degrees, on a beeline for San Francisco. The *Endiro Gotsu* had to be directly ahead. About two hundred miles out, give or take fifty miles.

Kai Tai's little chopper hummed satisfyingly as I cruised at four thousand feet. I kept an eye out for small planes or big jetliners that might be heading for Hiroshima or Seoul, or even Peking. And for military aircraft that might have been dispatched to intercept this Yankee on an unauthorized flight over international waters.

The sky was clear and empty. Luck rode with me there.

As I searched the now barren sea, my mind projected ahead, to what might happen when I eventually found the *Endiro Gotsu*.

Would the captain heed my warning to return to Japanese waters? I doubted it. Would the marksmen from the Sons of August Six, who now manned the freighter, shoot me down when I hovered close enough to use the bullhorn? It seemed very likely.

But I had to get close to the ship, even if I didn't broadcast a warning. I had no explosives to spare and I didn't dare try to drop any of them from a great height. As big as the average freighter is, it's difficult to hit from the air, unless you have well-designed bombs and a sophisticated system for delivery.

I had one distinct advantage over a military bomber, though. Even though I had no sophisticated system and would have to toss the explosives out of the cockpit by hand, at least I could choose a position above and just ahead of the ship and hover there until I did my part.

After that, the packets of explosives would be wholly dependent on gravity and on the whims of the wind.

But first, dangerous as it was, I had to give the captain a chance to turn back on his own.

In the back of my mind, though, was the ever-present thought that, no matter how successful I might be in turning the ship or blowing it out of the water, I didn't have enough fuel to make it to land, not even to the small offshore islands that dot the western Pacific near the coast of Japan.

If I didn't make it back, there was no way in hell to stop the Sons of August Six from pumping out more of those booby-trapped Tikki-Tik robots and shipping them to the States and to other countries allied with the States. I'd made a mistake zipping away from the factory the way I had. I should have dropped at least one of the boxes of explosives on the warehouse. Not only would that have slowed down the production of new robots, it would have forced some kind of action from authorities. Perhaps even have brought real investigators down from the office of the emperor. But I had been so certain I'd be back that I'd left the factory intact, going full tilt.

The loss of Nato Nakuma, the manager, would be a small loss to the Sons of August Six. They'd have a replacement running the operation before poor old Nakuma's body was cold.

Another thought came: Suppose there were storms ahead and the *Endiro Gotsu* had set a circling course to go north or south of them. I would run out all my fuel searching an empty sea.

All the worries and nagging thoughts began to gang up on me when after two hours of cruising at just over a hundred miles an hour, there was nothing but endless sea below.

I climbed to ten thousand feet, burning up precious fuel in the effort. Still, nothing ahead but empty sea.

Sweat was collecting in my armpits and streaking down my sides under my shirt. My kidneys began to ache, not only from my earlier beating, but because nature was putting out a warning that my bladder was ready to overflow.

I decided to continue on for another fifteen minutes, then to turn back if I hadn't spotted the ship. With luck, I figured on enough fuel to make it to a small, rocky island. If worse came to worst, I could build a hut out of clay and sticks, and live like a peasant on the sea's bounty.

Fourteen of those minutes went by with shattering speed. Even as I was glancing at my watch to check the time, I heard the small cough in the engine that warned me the main fuel tank was empty.

Quickly, I switched to the auxiliary tank on the right skid, the one that hadn't been damaged. The engine picked up and hummed along sweetly. For how long, I had no idea.

Fifteen minutes came and passed.

No ship. Just clear waters below.

Damn, to come so far, to come through so many rugged trials and traps and then to miss my target by miles, was just too damned much.

To hell with the fuel. I pulled back on the collective pitch, swept the skies with my eyes to make sure I wasn't climbing into the path of an oncoming plane, and rose to fifteen thousand feet. Then to eighteen.

It was suddenly cold in the cockpit, but I didn't

dare take my eyes off the sea below to look for the cabin heat switch. I cruised along at a hundred and twenty, sweeping the sea in all directions.

And there, behind me, several miles to the north, was a ship. I'd missed it coming east because the morning sun was in my eyes. But it could be any ship, not *the* ship.

Only one way to find out.

I dropped swiftly, on a collision course with the ship. As I neared, I saw that it was on a heading of seventy-eight degrees, that it flew a Japanese flag. I dropped almost to sea level and skimmed along the small, choppy waves, and made a pass from bow to stern.

There was the name, big and bold and clear: *Endiro Gotsu.*

I made a wide turn above the ship's choppy wake, slid back the bubble canopy and picked up the bullhorn. I closed in on the stern, where the bridge was located, and set my forward speed with the ship's. Thirty-six knots. She was a fast one. No wonder she'd gone farther than I'd calculated.

I saw men with rifles, spread out across the deck and on the different levels of the bridge.

"Ahoy *Endiro Gotsu*," I called out through the bullhorn. "I must speak with your captain. I have no radio. Please respond by bullhorn."

I watched the riflemen. If I saw a single tongue of flame, I'd pull away, climb to an advantageous position and drop all three boxes of explosives. I was through screwing around. Just this one warning and then—doomsday.

No one fired. I was preparing to repeat my message, holding aloft at only a hundred yards, when a short, stocky man in a crisp blue uniform came out of the wheelhouse with a bullhorn. He leaned against the railing on the narrow catwalk.

"Ahoy, helicopter. What is it you wish?"

In as few words as possible, I gave the warning. I told the captain I knew that his crew was made up of members of the Sons of August Six, that the robot toys bound for San Francisco were all filled with TNT and timers to go off on Christmas day. I told him that I was fully prepared to blow him out of the sea if he didn't turn the ship around and head back for Hiroshima.

Raucous laughter wafted up from the ship.

And then I saw the tongues of flame.

The first bullet to reach me caught the bullhorn and knocked it out of my hands. It whizzed away to the rear and fell into the ocean. Other bullets whined above my head.

I worked every control at once, climbing, swerving to the right, picking up speed.

When I was at five thousand feet, well in front of the ship—and well beyond fire range of the M-16s—I made my strike plans.

It was impossible to toss out all three boxes at once. And I knew that it would take at least all three to penetrate the steel decks of the freighter and set off the TNT in all those Tikki-Tik robots.

What I needed, I decided, was a bombardier, someone to collect all the packets in one lump and drop it on the ship while I held the copter in place.

Well, I was the pilot *and* bombardier on this run.

Maybe there was a way.

I checked the boxes and found that the packets were placed in individual pockets of styrofoam. The styrofoam took up most of the room in each box.

Working as swiftly as possible and still keeping the chopper ahead of the ship, I repacked the TNT packets, tossing the styrofoam out over the side. I saw that the wind currents were just perfect. The light styrofoam floated down toward the ship.

When they landed on the deck, the crewmen thought they were some kind of lightweight bombs. They all scurried to get out of the way. The only problem was, there was no place to go to get out of the way, except into the sea.

Next, I tossed out the two spare boxes and watched them float down and terrify the crewmen once more. Gingerly, knowing that I was now working with a box of highly dangerous cargo that could explode at the slightest jar, I worked the box up over the side of the cockpit.

I checked my position in relation to the ship. Perfect. Even as I was pushing the boxload of TNT overboard, I had a sudden thought that it might hit the skid below and blow me up like the pesky gnat I had become to the men below.

I was so concerned about the trajectory of this third and final load that I forgot to increase throttle and get the hell out of there.

I watched, fascinated, as the box streaked down through the sky, from a thousand feet up, on a deadly collision course with the ship. The box cleared the bow and was dropping about midships when I suddenly realized what would happen next.

I was a bit late.

The controls worked smoothly in my hands and I was already making a hard turn, and climbing rapidly, when the explosion came. I looked back and saw the fireball, saw men leaping into the sea, saw the captain on his bridge shaking his fist at me.

In rapid fire, several explosions rocked the ship from bow to stern. I could feel the concussion buffeting the chopper, could feel the heat from the blasts.

And then came the finale.

A crashing boom louder than anything I had ever heard rent the air around me. I was in the center of a hell-fire blast that seemed to go on forever.

The immense wave of concussion whipped the chopper like a hickory switch whips a mischievous child. I felt the helicopter being flipped over on its side. As it tipped, its rotors flailing helplessly against the air, I caught a glimpse of the holocaust below, and felt something strike me in the head.

An incredible fireball had risen from the ship and was shooting smoke and fire high into the air—ten thousand feet up.

I worked furiously on the controls, hitting top throttle, but the furious concussive winds still had the chopper in their control. I felt the little sky-ship nose over and was looking down at the ocean surface.

Already, a massive tidal wave was moving out from the site of the explosion, building in height and strength.

I saw struggling bodies—and unstruggling parts of bodies—in that massive wave.

The sound seemed to go on forever. And the heat.

It wasn't until I had the ship more or less under control that I felt the trickle of blood down my face and felt the pain in my head and back. I had been bouncing around in the cockpit like a numbered ball in a bingo cage.

My hands trembled on the twin controls of the helicopter as I made a final sweep of the *Endiro Gotsu*. There was nothing left but an immense black spot. The ship was gone. The tidal wave was rushing away from the black spot in a three-hundred-sixty-degree arc.

The Bell engine was coughing and spitting, so I turned to the second auxiliary tank and was surprised when the engine caught and began once more to purr the way an engine should purr. But the controls felt sloppy. The chopper didn't respond the way it should, and the tail kept swinging from side to side.

I looked back and saw why. The stabilizer rotor was gone. Not merely twisted, but gone.

The blood seemed to be coming faster now, getting into my eyes. I wiped it away and probed the head wound with my fingers. There was something sharp jutting from my skin. I pulled it out and the blood gushed. I hadn't bumped my head during those rolling concussions; a hunk of metal from the ship had embedded itself in my skull. I guessed that a part of it was still lodged in the bone.

I controlled a growing panic and set a course for two hundred seventy degrees, heading directly for Hiroshima. The helicopter swayed and bucked, but it stayed mostly on course.

For a few miles.

Ten minutes after I'd left the black spot on the ocean where the *Endiro Gotsu* had been, the engine began to cough again. I revved up the throttle, but that only seemed to make the engine angrier.

It coughed twice more, then died with a loud clatter.

The engine, no doubt, had picked up some shrapnel from the ship, the same as I had. That, plus the hole in the left auxiliary tank, had been too much for it.

All I could think of as the chopper fluttered like a crippled butterfly toward the ocean surface below was that it had almost been worth it to have seen that series of tremendous explosions.

TWENTY–SEVEN

I never felt the impact when the little chopper wafted into the ocean. And, the next several minutes were strange, indeed. I was floating at first—I mean, floating on air—feeling euphoric and at peace with the world. Then, I was choking on seawater, flailing. Finally, I felt myself sinking and was unable to use my arms to keep me on the ocean's surface.

Suddenly, I felt hands pulling me from the depth of the salty water, felt myself being hoisted into the air and into a warm place. I heard the throb and roar of a powerful engine, felt the headiness of being lifted into the air. Blackness, then soft light and the lovely face.

Nashima.

Behind her, peering over her shoulder with concern on her pretty face, was Kiko.

Nashima was doing something to my head, just above my eyes. I felt pressure and pain there, then the comfortable feel of cloth. Nashima had taken off her blouse and was bandaging my wound with it.

At that time, I came fully awake. I didn't have to ask where I was. I could see Kai Tai's head and shoulders in the pilot's seat ahead. I was lying on a narrow couch at the rear of the cockpit. We were in Kai Tai's clipper ship. But how had Nashima arranged all this?

I tried to talk, to sit up. Nashima shushed me with a gentle finger to my lips and a firm push to my shoulders.

"We'll get you to the hospital, Nick," she said softly. "You're pale from loss of blood. And then Kiko and I have a surprise for you. Don't talk now. Don't try to get up."

"But what's going on? What's . . ."

"Never mind," she said. "Don't talk. Just blink in answer to my next question. Blink once for yes, twice for no. Did you stop the *Endiro Gotsu?*"

I forgot how many times I was supposed to blink. My mind was still foggy.

"I stopped it," I said. "My God, you should have seen and heard—"

"Shush," she said, the finger back to my lips. "Now, you listen to what we've done."

Nashima had talked with her father after I'd left, telling him about her brother's death. The old man had said it was time to stop being afraid of the Sons of August Six, time to fight back against the threat.

Using intel I'd given her on the positions of the guards outside, Nashima had organized search-

and-destroy parties. She and her relatives had gone out and killed all twenty-six guards surrounding the Porfiro mansion.

Next, she'd called the Imperial Palace and talked with the head of the Japanese Secret Service. The man was an old friend of Nashima's father. They decided they'd have to trust him.

"I told him about the hidious plan of the Sons of August Six," she said, "about the enormous Christmas kill they hoped to achieve in America. I told him of our unsuccessful efforts to halt production and have Nato Nakuma arrested. I told him of the way the police refused to cooperate."

Her trust in the man proved worthwhile. Within the hour, contingents of the Japanese Secret Service took over the local police force, established Nashima's relatives in the factory, halted the loading of ships and confiscated all the explosive packets.

From that, I deduced, the robots would still reach their destination. Not the ones I'd blown up in that horrendous and fascinating explosion at sea, but the remaining ones—and the ones to be produced in the future.

I slipped out of consciousness for a time, then floated back into it. The pains were returning, so I knew that I wouldn't remain in my euphoric state much longer.

"I have to call Hawk," I said. "He has to know . . ."

"He has been called," Nashima said. "I will call again to say that you are alive, but you have no reporting to do now. Not for a long time. For you, there is the hospital. And then . . ."

She stopped. She and Kiko were smiling in that quaint, enigmatic, Oriental way.

"And then what?" I asked.

DON'T MISS THE NEXT NEW
NICK CARTER SPY THRILLER

THE GREEK SUMMIT

We were only about a block from Syntagma, or Constitution Square. From there it was a short walk to the Plaka, probably the liveliest part of Athens.

"When the conference starts," I said, "and your husband is behind closed doors for a few hours, I'll take you out again. You can do some shopping and we can have lunch in a taverna."

"That'll be lovely," she said.

"We'd better get back." I said.

About a block from the hotel I stopped, pulling her into a doorway. "What's going on, Sherry? What's with you and Johns? Do you love the guy, or what?"

"Nick, don't—" she said, turning her head away, but I grabbed her by the shoulders and made her face me.

"What's wrong with him?" I asked, letting her

shoulders go. "Not only does he never talk to you, he never touches you. If I was married to you, I wouldn't be able to keep my hands off of you."

She stared into my face then and said, "If only you were married to me, Nick."

She was so close, I could feel her breath on my face. I put my arms around her, pulled her closer and kissed her. Her mouth was hot beneath mine, willing.

"Nick—" she started to say, pulling her mouth away, and that's when they hit us.

There were three of them; when one of the trio grabbed for Sherry I didn't waste any time. I flicked my wrist and Hugo jumped into my hand. I slashed her assailant's face, and he fell back. A second man moved in and threw a punch which glanced off my shoulder. I kicked out and caught him on the knee, driving him back as well.

I told Sherry to stay inside the doorway, but I moved out. The man I'd slashed was on one knee, trying to keep his face from falling off. The other two came back at me, but they didn't know how to approach the knife. They weren't pros, and for that reason I left Wilhelmina where she was, safe and snug beneath my left arm.

"Come on," I said to them, not knowing whether they could understand me or not. They were both watching the knife, so I stepped in and struck with my left hand while they watched Hugo in my right.

I hit the gimpy one flush on the face with my left fist and he fell backward. The other one had the presence of mind to throw a kick at me. I turned and took it on my thigh, but I felt the shock of it down my leg.

He was in close at that point and I could have driven Hugo right through his sternum, but I didn't want to kill him. I reached out and took off a small piece of his chin, and he clasped his hands to his face and howled. It was the gimpy one who shouted something to the other two, and they all took off down the street.

—From THE GREEK SUMMIT
A New Nick Carter Spy Thriller
From Ace Charter in February

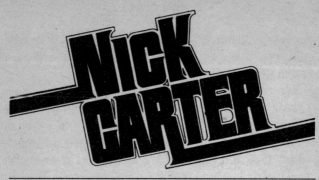

☐ 15870-1	**DOOMSDAY SPORE**	$1.75
☐ 17014-5	**THE DUBROVNIK MASSACRE**	$2.25
☐ 18124-4	**EARTH SHAKER**	$2.50
☐ 29782-X	**THE GOLDEN BULL**	$2.25
☐ 34909-9	**THE HUMAN TIME BOMB**	$2.25
☐ 34999-4	**THE HUNTER**	$2.50
☐ 35868-3	**THE INCA DEATH SQUAD**	$2.50
☐ 35881-0	**THE ISRAELI CONNECTION**	$2.50
☐ 43201-8	**KATMANDU CONTRACT**	$2.25
☐ 47183-8	**THE LAST SAMURAI**	$2.50
☐ 58866-2	**NORWEGIAN TYPHOON**	$2.50
☐ 64053-2	**THE OMEGA TERROR**	$1.95
☐ 63400-1	**OPERATION: McMURDO SOUND**	$2.50
☐ 64426-0	**THE OUSTER CONSPIRACY**	$2.25

Available wherever paperbacks are sold or use this coupon.

Ⓒ ACE CHARTER BOOKS
P.O. Box 400, Kirkwood, N.Y. 13795

Please send me the titles checked above. I enclose $_____
Include $1.00 per copy for postage and handling. Send check or
money order only. New York State residents please add sales tax.

NAME_____

ADDRESS_____

CITY_____STATE_____ZIP_____